Black Horse
Gena Gendusa LaSalle

ISBN: 979-8-9919004-2-3 (pb)

ISBN: 979-8-9919004-3-0 (ebook)

Library of Congress Control Number: 2025909705

Book Cover by Gena Gendusa LaSalle and Canva Designs

1st edition 2025

www.gglbooks.com

To my husband, who let me use
all his words and ideas,
and to Sharlette and Jenny for
making it through the beginning.

"The love of power is the demon of mankind."

Friedrich Nietzsche

Prologue

December 19, 1998

The black horse raced across the lush, overgrown pasture. I wasn't riding on its back, though. Instead, we were running side by side. I could see his beautiful, coal-colored coat shimmering in the sunlight as he galloped gracefully alongside me. In the next moment, he took one look at me—I could've sworn he winked at me—and began running even faster ahead of me, turning into a blur far into the distance.

I tried unsuccessfully to catch up to him. Right when I thought I was making progress, I woke up to my alarm clock ringing in my ear and my heart pounding.

I briefly remembered having this same dream two other times recently, and I was beginning to think that maybe it was a sign, or the universe was trying to tell me something. Although, I never really believed in stuff like that, so why start now?

"And you're just running with this horse, in a field, and then he winks at you and disappears?" Ashley, my roommate, asked me eagerly after I finished explaining the dream to her later that morning. Unlike me, she *did* believe in things like this having a deeper meaning.

"Yes, but you know I don't believe in all that mumbo jumbo about dreams trying to tell you something," I said unconvincingly. "It is weird that I've had the same dream three times now, right?"

"I have this book that interprets dreams—"

"No, absolutely not!" I cut her off, feeling silly for thinking it was anything more than just a dream.

"Suit yourself," she said with a smirk on her face.

Ashley left later that morning to go shopping for some last-minute Christmas gifts, while I stayed behind to get some work done.

I couldn't stop thinking about the dream. After working for a couple of hours, I stood up from the kitchen table and stretched, my muscles stiff from sitting for so long, and eyed the open door to Ashley's room. I snuck in and found a dream book sitting on top of a stack of other books on her nightstand.

I sat on the couch and began flipping through the pages in search of any information as to what a black horse running through a field meant, feeling idiotic all the while.

Before I could find anything, Ashley opened the door and walked in, loaded down with bags from Bloomingdale's, Macy's, and another store I'd never heard of. She laughed as she caught me hastily tossing the book on the coffee table.

"Couldn't resist, could you?" she asked, still laughing as she went into her room to put her bags down.

"Maybe I was just a little curious," I said coolly. I felt slightly embarrassed that I got caught.

Ashley came back out of her room and sat down on the couch next to me with another book in her hand called *Dreams: Good and Bad Omens.*

"Well, I already looked for you before I left earlier because I wanted to know," she said as she flipped through the book. "It was in this book, not that one. Here we go. It says, 'Black horses are carriers of positive energy that may be entering your life soon. While it may not be obvious at first, this energy will have a positive effect on you. Black horses are also a sign of your strong ability to overcome obstacles.' Blah, blah,

blah…" she paused her reading to skim through and locate a specific passage.

"Oh here's the other part that I found interesting," she said. "'Black horses can symbolize death, but not in the literal sense. In some cases, it can mean leaving behind things which no longer serve you. Or rather, death and rebirth; the closing of one door and the opening of another. This is a powerful omen of bold transformation. While you may be attached to your current habits, relationships, ideas, and plans, it may be time to strip away your old ideals and embrace new ones.'" She finished reading the excerpt from her book and stared at me wide-eyed with excitement.

"So, something new is coming, and it'll be good, but it will change my life and make me leave behind everything I know…?" I reiterated aloud, mostly to myself.

"That's what it sounds like!" she said, snapping the book closed. "Maybe you're going to meet the perfect man soon!"

"Right," I said sarcastically, "or maybe that author is just really good at making up stories that make you believe things that aren't true, which is what writers do. Dreams are nothing more than a compilation of random images that we've seen before, and that's all."

"Don't be such a skeptic! You'll be sorry when the book turns out to be right."

"Whatever you say," I said, hoping she would let it go.

Luckily she changed the subject by asking, "Are you excited for your birthday in a couple of weeks?"

ONE

I've always heard that your thirties are your golden years, the time when you begin to feel older and wiser. As if going from twenty-nine to thirty in one second at midnight changes everything about you and how you view the world. Most women that I knew dreaded their thirties because of what comes next—the loss of their youth and the journey to their forties. I guess I'm different... I looked forward to turning thirty tomorrow. My twenties were great and had treated me well, but I was excited to see what the next decade would bring.

The eve of my birthday was also New Year's Eve, which, according to Ashley, my best friend and roommate, meant that we needed to have a big night out on the town in celebration of both occasions. She had assured me multiple times over the last few weeks that she had planned the entire night out perfectly, and while I tried begging several times to stay in, she declined my request each time. I felt that going out in Manhattan on New Year's Eve was mostly for rookies and tourists.

"Are you sure we can't stay in like we always do?" I asked one more time, hoping she would change her mind. "We can watch the ball drop on TV in our pajamas with a bottle of cheap champagne. It's just another birthday, ya know?"

"Absolutely not missy. You're not weaseling your way out of this one. Don't get me wrong; I love our little New Year's

Eve tradition, but it's been a while since we went out on the town to ring in a new year. Plus, thirty *is* a big deal!" she insisted with the same reasoning that she kept giving me all week.

She was excited, so I decided not to try and persuade her to stay in anymore. It was inevitable; we were going out.

"Well, this old lady needs a nap before we go out... What time did you want to leave, and what's our first stop again?"

"Sheesh, not even thirty yet, and you're pulling the old lady card." Ashley crossed her arms and rolled her eyes. "Fine, go rest, Grandma. We're starting at Johnny's place at nine-thirty."

I laughed as I walked into my room. Life in New York changed after I had met Ashley three and a half years ago. I had just been promoted to manager of my first team at the market consulting firm, Greenhouse Inc., when Ashley, a high-spirited redhead fresh out of college, took the intern position on my team. We were the only two people in our division who weren't natives of New York City. She was from a small town outside of Columbus, Ohio, called Jorge Town, and I was from Lakeshore, Texas, also a small town, on the outskirts of Lubbock.

Ashley was a petite girl with a big personality, and though she was a few years younger than me, she was more mature than most of the other women my age who I'd met in New York. She'd confided in me before about having to grow up at a young age after her mom died when she was only eleven years old. Her big brown eyes, bright smile, and long, fiery red locks would've fooled anyone of her troubled past and instead turned heads when she walked into a room. However, she was always convinced that people were looking at me instead.

A few hours later, Ashley sat on my bed in a short, tight, sparkly black dress, with stilettos that made her as tall as me, while I examined myself in the mirror hanging on my wall. I changed six times before deciding on a chic, long-sleeved, low-cut red dress that fell right above my knee.

Ashley gave my cleavage hanging out of the front a thumbs up, said it was a 'good thing', and I wasn't allowed to change again.

I pinned half of my hair up to keep it out of my face and let the rest of the long, dark curls fall down my back.

"You look great," I heard Ashley say behind me. "Now, can we go?"

"Yes, let's go!"

We made our way to the first stop of the night, a little hole in the wall bar on the same block as our apartment called Johnny's Pub. It was named after the owner, Johnny De Luca. We had frequented his place so much since moving to the Upper West Side that Johnny considered us to be regulars in the bar.

"Well, hello there, ladies!" Johnny shouted from across the bar as soon as we walked through the door. "No pajamas and cheap champagne tonight?"

"Hey Johnny!" we said at the same time, then Ashley added with a big smile on her face, "And no, I was finally able to get Riley to dress up for a night out on the town. Can we get the usual, please?"

"And an order of mozzarella sticks, pretty please?" I asked.

Ashley shot me a look of disapproval.

"What?! I'm hungry!"

"Come on, Ashley," said Johnny. "Whatever the birthday girl wants, the birthday girl gets." He also noticed her disapproving stare.

Johnny had become somewhat of a big brother to us after seeing us studying a tourist map of Manhattan the first time that we had come in to eat. We spent all day moving into the apartment and were trying to figure out how to get to

Greenwich Village. He tossed our map in the garbage and spent three hours giving us the *low down*—as he worded it—of the city.

I liked Johnny. He was shorter than the average man with dense, curly, greased-backed hair, dark, beady eyes, and a big nose in the middle of his face. Ashley and I joked during one of our movie nights that he looked like Sonny from *Grease*. He was also a vicious flirt with all the women who came into his bar, including Ashley and me. His muscles bulged out of the sleeves of the tight, black T-shirts that he always wore. Even though he could take home any woman he pursued, he remained a true gentleman in that he had one rule for himself: he would not sleep with any patrons of the bar.

"It's not my birthday yet—"

"But we will take any freebies that you're willing to offer!" Ashley interrupted as she grabbed both our drinks from him and winked.

"Anything for my favorite customers." He smiled and left to help another customer who had come in behind us.

We sat at the end of the bar and talked for a while, enjoying my mozzarella sticks and watching as the crowd grew larger as the time creeped closer to midnight. We recognized a few other people who also frequented Johnny's bar almost as much as we did, but the rest were strangers, looking for a place to celebrate New Year's far away from the hoard of people in Times Square.

"You ladies need another drink?" Johnny had come over to check on us in between taking drink orders.

"I can't believe you even feel the need to ask, Jonathan!" Ashley joked.

After bringing us another round he asked, "What's the big plans for tonight?"

"We are heading to Nate's after these drinks for his big New Year's Eve party." Ashley paused to take a sip, unaware of the annoyed look that Johnny and I shared briefly. Then she continued, "His apartment has a great view of Time's Square, so I thought for Riley's birthday she could watch the ball drop in person instead of on the TV."

I believed that she was thinking of me being able to see Time's Square from his balcony when Nate invited her to his party—the first of his parties that he'd ever invited her to since they met—but I knew the real reason behind her plan for us to go to this party tonight. Nate Cumberland was the son of Mitch Cumberland, the owner and CEO of Cumberland Financials, the largest financing company in the Northeast. They met at the gym shortly after she moved to the city, and she quickly fell head over heels for his good looks and rich boy charm. Unlike her, I saw right through him for the player he was as he usually only called when it was convenient for him or late at night when no one else answered the phone.

I suspected that deep down she was hoping tonight would be the night that Nate would make it official and ask her to be his girlfriend after sharing a midnight kiss, but I knew better.

We paid and waved goodbye to Johnny after finishing our drinks and headed to the street to call a taxi.

"How many people are supposed to be at this party?" I asked Ashley as we slid into the back of the cab.

"Nate said a few people from the gym and some guys he went to high school with," she responded cheerfully. "He really does have a great view of Times Square!"

"Yes, so I've heard." I shook my head and turned to look out the window for a quick glimpse of Central Park. It was one of my favorite places in New York, especially at this time of the year with all the lights decorated in the trees. The air was cold tonight, making me wish I'd brought a heavier coat, but it wasn't supposed to snow, so I thought maybe we'd be fine, especially once we got inside the apartment.

"If you don't want to go, we can go back to Johnny's," Ashley said with a sad look on her face.

I would've loved nothing more than to stay at Johnny's, or be at home in my sweats, but even I had to admit, it was nice getting dressed up and out of the house.

"No, it's fine. I'm excited!" I replied. "This will be my first time watching the ball drop in person since I moved here."

Her frown quickly turned back into a grin as she faced back forward. "Good!"

Nate's apartment was located between 6th Avenue and West 42nd Street. We stepped out of the taxi and were greeted by a tall doorman who pointed us in the direction of the lobby. Inside, the main entrance was decadent, covered in black and cream-colored marble with accents of gold within the furniture and rugs. We stepped into the elevator, where Ashley pressed forty-nine on the number board—the floor right below the penthouse.

Before the doors opened to Nate's floor, we could hear the music from the party taking over the elevator tune.

"I thought you said this was going to be a *small* party?"

Ashley shrugged. "That's what Nate told me."

The doors opened to reveal a long hallway leading to a burly bouncer standing guard at the main entrance. He let us pass without question as to who we were or if we had an invitation.

There were at least fifty people jam-packed into Nate's apartment, which luckily, from what I could see, was a very spacious flat. The living room and kitchen all flowed into one room and both were all white except for the black appliances and couches. On the walls were a series of large red paintings, the kind that looked like an artist spilled buckets of paint all over them. There was a large, electric fireplace on the wall to the left, which had a fire blazing steadily. The middle of each room had a set of glass French doors leading out to a balcony overlooking the city.

"This place is amazing!" I yelled at Ashley over the noise of the crowd.

"What?!" she shouted back.

The DJ and his speakers were right next to the door, making it impossible to have a conversation.

"Let's go find the bar!" Ashley shouted again, this time closer to my ear.

We pushed through the crowd to the bar that was set up on the other side of the kitchen. Rich kids really didn't skimp on their parties, I thought to myself. Nate hired a bouncer, DJ, and a mini bar—bartender included—for his New Year's Eve bash.

"Two beers please," Ashley asked the bartender politely. The music was still loud, but it was much quieter on this side of the room. Once we were handed our beers, I motioned toward the open doors leading to the balcony, and Ashley led the way.

Two

There were less people on the balcony, which I wasn't upset about, although it was most likely the chilly breeze keeping them away. However, the view of the city and Times Square was incredible.

"Hey! Ashley!" someone called from the far end of the balcony.

Ashley turned to see who called her name and smiled with a smile that only I was trained to know was her fake, I-don't-like-you smile. "Hey, Natalie! I thought you weren't going to be able to make it."

"My other plans—well, let's just say they were cancelled," Natalie said with a shrug. "This is Joey. Joey, this is Ashley. We go to the same gym."

It hit me suddenly that I remembered Ashley telling me about a Natalie from the gym, a girl who was always doting over Nate. Ashley couldn't stand her and often described Natalie as being patronizing.

She was built similarly to Ashley, small and fit, except instead of having long, fiery red locks like Ashley, her dull brown hair was straight and cut short. Natalie was pretty, with a small round face and dark eyes. Joey looked as if he could be Natalie's twin brother as he had the same plain facial features, but with a bald head, and he wore thin-rimmed eyeglasses.

"Joey is my cousin," said Natalie.

That made sense too, I thought.

"And he just started an internship at *Margo*," added Natalie.

"Nice to meet you," Joey said enthusiastically, then turned to me with his hand extended. "And you are?"

"This is Riley, my roommate," Ashley cut in before I could introduce myself.

"Hi," I said as I took his hand. "*Margo*, huh? That's exciting. It's becoming a very big magazine in the fashion industry."

"Yes, it's very exciting! I am getting to work under some of the biggest up-and-coming fashion designers," Joey answered eagerly.

"That's great! Natalie, what do you do?" I acted as if I didn't notice Ashley glaring at me for trying to get to know her archnemesis.

"I have one more semester at Columbia before I graduate from law school."

As Natalie continued to discuss her job prospects at law firms—I could see now why Ashley thought she was patronizing—Ashley disappeared, most likely to go track down Nate, leaving me alone with Natalie and Joey.

Once Natalie finished, she asked me, "How do you and Ashley know one another?"

"She's on the team that I manage at Greenhouse Inc. We create and manage advertisements for clients. When she came onto my team, she was new to the city and needed a place to live and my lease was up. We moved in and have been friends ever since," I answered.

"That's awesome! Joey and I grew up outside of town but came to the city every day. We both moved here as soon as we were old enough to get our own place," she said as she finished her drink. She glanced at her watch, then at Joey. "I'm going to get another drink, want anything?"

Joey shook his head, and she left. He and I continued talking about work and living in the city. Joey didn't seem to mind that Natalie never returned. I felt bad leaving him there alone, but I wanted to go and check on Ashley and find a bathroom.

I managed to find the bathroom, but not Ashley, and by the time I returned, Joey was gone. I stood near the edge of the balcony watching the crowd below, which from this height looked like a large group of frantic ants running back and forth through Times Square. It was getting close to midnight, and I wondered how much longer we would be here when I heard Ashley come up behind me.

"Riley! Look who I found... this is Mark. He went to high school with Nate." She leaned closer to me and whispered, "And he is very single at the moment." She stood back up and continued in her normal voice, "Mark, this is Riley. I think you two should talk, for, oh, I don't know, the next few minutes or so," she said as she glanced at the non-existent watch on her wrist. Then she disappeared as quickly as she had arrived.

We both stood there, smiling at one another after our awkward and hasty introduction.

"Hi," he said as he extended his hand. "Riley, was it?"

"Yes, hi," I said with a small laugh. I took his hand to shake it, which was warm and inviting on this chilly night.

"How is your night so far?"

"I can't complain. I've got a cold beer and a great view of the ball dropping in Times Square."

"Oh yeah, I forgot that we can see that from Nate's apartment."

"How could you forget about it? It's right there!" I said pointing down below.

Mark was tall, and although he was wearing a jacket, I could tell he was built like an athlete. I didn't take him to be a gym rat like Ashley and Nate though. He had whiskey-colored eyes and smoothed back chestnut brown hair.

"I know," he said, smirking enough to reveal a small dimple in the side of his cheek, "but if you've seen it once, you've seen it a hundred times."

"Spoken like a truly cynical New Yorker."

"Come on, give me a break. Do you really find it *that* exciting?"

"Yes. Well, no. I don't know. I find it mesmerizing, or at least I did when I was a kid. Then again, I didn't grow up watching it every year in person," I defended myself. "Plus, the thousands of people that are attracted to it every year would disagree with you, too."

"Maybe you have a point. Although the traffic should be enough to make you want to outlaw it," he joked.

"You're ruining one of my favorite parts about New York," I answered sarcastically, thinking he wasn't wrong about that part. However, it was New York, and there was always traffic.

"What did you do on New Year's Eve if you didn't spend it watching a small ball float down a flagpole?" he asked.

I laughed as I thought back to the first time I arrived in New York and how extremely disappointed and shocked I was when I finally spotted the infamous ball on top of the building. It was so much smaller than I expected that I'd almost missed it.

"My parents threw these huge parties where we would light a giant bonfire in our back pasture and set off fireworks all night long. It was the only night of the year that I was allowed to stay up past my bedtime," I said proudly.

"Oh yeah, and what third-world country is that?"

"Ha ha, very funny." I took a sip of my beer before answering. "That third world country would be called Texas. Ever heard of it?"

"I think so... that's the big one at the bottom of the map, right?" His dimple showed itself again before he said, "I'm kidding. I can see it though; I thought I heard a little bit of an accent."

"Me? I'm not the one with an accent, you are!"

He laughed aloud and added, "How did you end up here in New York?"

I told him the abridged version of always wanting to move here when I was younger and how I finally got my chance when I was accepted into Yale's business school program. "It wasn't New York obviously, but it was closer than I had been. After graduating, I sought out jobs in the city and now here I am, four and a half years later."

"Nice. Where do you work?"

"Greenhouse Inc."

"That's a very reputable company—impressive. I guess that's how you and Ashley know each other... doesn't she work there too?" he asked.

"Yes, she's actually on the team that I manage," I answered. "And she's also my roommate."

"Lucky you."

I noted a hint of sarcasm in his voice. "She's not that bad." I pushed his shoulder in a playful way. "She's a great friend and a good person. She got me out for my birthday tonight."

"What?! Happy birthday!" he said. "Can I get the birthday girl another drink?"

"I'm okay for now but thank you." I smiled. "Should be getting close to midnight now anyway. I'm sure you want to get back to your friends." I didn't really want him to go, but I was sure he didn't want to be hanging around here when the countdown started.

He checked his watch and looked at me. "Ten minutes till midnight... I've got nowhere else to be, and I haven't even told you what I do for a living yet."

Good, I thought to myself, he doesn't want to go either. "You're right. How rude of me? What *do* you do for a living, Mark?"

"I'm a spoiled, rich, trust fund kid who mooches off his parents' money, lying around all day while my butlers serve me endlessly," he answered with a straight face.

"That's..." I started and paused, not knowing how to respond to him, "cool, I guess."

He smirked, and before he could say anything, I said, "You're joking with me, aren't you?"

"Yes, I am." He smiled big enough to show a set of perfect white teeth this time and took a sip of the beer in his hand before adding, "I work for my father at his company, Madison Financials. He insists that I learn the family business."

Madison Financials was more than a mom-and-pop financial company. I'd recently read that they were in the top twenty-five ranking of Fortune 500 companies in the world. He didn't sound excited about his prospects of getting into the family business though.

"That's one of the top financials companies in the world, from what I've read."

"Yes, it is. It's every kid's dream to grow up and run a Fortune 500 company."

"I take it that it's not your dream though?" I paused and then asked, "What is your dream then?"

He looked surprised, like he'd never been asked that before. He thought about his answer for a second and finally responded with, "To be a spoiled, rich, trust fund kid who mooches off his parents' money and lies around all day while my butlers serve me endlessly."

We were both laughing before he could finish the part about butlers serving him endlessly, catching the attention of a group of girls standing nearby. He stopped and added, "I'm kidding—for the most part. If I'm being honest, I'd rather be doing something that I'm passionate about. I know my dad's company would be an easy out for success, but it's not something that I really care for, if you know what I mean."

I did know what he meant; marketing wasn't necessarily my dream come true, but living in New York City was my dream for now, and my career made that possible.

I didn't get a chance to respond because a loud voice from inside shouted, "Two minutes until midnight, everyone!"

"Well, Riley," he said my name slowly, like he was savoring it, "can I call you sometime after tonight?"

"I'd like that," I said and reached into my handbag for one of my business cards and a pen. I wrote my number on the back and handed it to him as the crowd began to shout, "TEN, NINE, EIGHT..."

"Almost time," Mark started. "Would you do me the honor of being my midnight kiss?"

"...SIX, FIVE..."

"Of course I would," I said, the corner of my mouth twitching into a grin, thinking to myself that I'd be more than happy to kiss him. His eyes were fixed on me, and I didn't care that I was missing the ball drop down below us.

"THREE... TWO... ONE... HAPPY NEW YEAR!" The crowd inside, along with the ones who had ventured out to the balcony, all bellowed at once.

At the same time, Mark leaned in for a kiss, and not just for a quick New Year's Eve peck. We stayed interlocked for what seemed like several minutes, his lips soft and warm against mine.

When we finally parted, the excitement from the crowd had died down and I heard him say, *Damn, she's hot. I wonder if she'd let me kiss her again.*

Or so I thought it was Mark that had said it, but his bright eyes were intent on me and his lips hadn't moved, so I figured it was someone behind us who wanted more of a midnight kiss than they had received.

Mark placed his hand on the back of my head and pulled me toward him before I could investigate. This time he kissed me more passionately, and the fireworks still going off in the background made the moment feel like the ending to a happy romance movie. I ran my hands up his back underneath his jacket, his heat resonating onto me.

Then he said, *My God, her hands are freezing!*

"Sorry!" I whispered in between kisses.

"You've got nothing to be sorry about," he replied, also in between a kiss.

After several minutes, I pushed him away, remembering where I was and who I'd come with, and the fact that I hadn't seen Ashley in a while.

"Everything okay?" he asked, then I thought heard him say, *Is she not as into this as I thought she was?*

"No, I am, the kiss was great—amazing even," I said a little out of breath. "I should probably go and find Ashley though and wish her a Happy New Year."

"Oh, right." He looked disappointed, but I wasn't leaving this party with anyone other than Ashley, no matter how hot they were or how great of a kisser they were.

Going to tell her about the amazing kiss you just had, huh?

"Something like that," I joked, and his facial expression changed from disappointment to confusion very quickly. "I look forward to that call sometime... Happy New Year, Mark."

"Happy New Year, Riley."

THREE

I pushed my way through what was now an even louder crowd than when we first arrived in search of Ashley. I was excited, tired, and ready to go home. I found her sitting alone by the bar with an upset look on her face.

She looked up as I approached her—that's when I noticed her eyes were red and puffy. Oh no, I thought to myself, What did Nate do now?

"Hey, let's go home," I shouted to her over the noise of the crowd.

She nodded her head, chugged what was left of her drink, and stormed out without glancing behind her to make sure I was following.

The noise level decreased tremendously once we were back in the hallway, and I could hear Ashley muttering to herself, *I am so stupid. I cannot believe I let this happen again. Riley was right all along.*

As she was reaching for the button to call the elevator I said, "Ashley, what's wrong? What was I right about?"

She stopped, finger suspended in front of the button, and turned slowly to look at me, eyes round as if she were seeing a ghost. I was nervous, thinking for a second that maybe she'd been drugged. When she didn't answer, I asked again, "What's wrong? What happened?"

She continued to stare at me as if I were the crazy one right now. Finally, as she turned back around and hit the button, she said, "Nothing. I'll tell you about it later." She stood there for a moment waiting before I heard in a whispered tone, *Did I say that out loud? How strange...*

I was too exhausted for her games, so I let it go and figured she would tell me later once she had time to cool down. Thankfully, the elevator arrived seconds later.

Halfway down the elevator ride, she started again on her rant.

Maybe she's had too much to drink? Maybe I've had too much to drink! And freaking Nate, what the hell is wrong with him?

I turned on her and shouted, "I've only had two drinks since we got here! What is the matter with you?!"

"Okay, good for you," she answered even more irritated than I was. "Nothing is wrong! I'm fine!"

I couldn't believe her. She's the one who ditched me to follow Nate around like a sad little puppy, and he probably blew her off as he always did. Now she was taking it out on me. We didn't say another word to each other until we got into the cab, and I wished her a happy New Year.

"Yeah, happy New Year... and happy birthday."

The rest of the ride home was silent—except for the inappropriate comments that the cab driver was directing toward us.

I love working New Year's Eve when all the beautiful girls come out to play in their skimpy little dresses. These two look feisty...

I looked at Ashley in disbelief because she was sitting there, staring out the window. Typically, when we came across a rude cab driver, she would be shouting threats of cutting their balls off, but this time, nothing.

I wonder what it would be like to have both of them at once.

I did my best to ignore him as Ashley was doing. Twenty long minutes later, we were back at the apartment. Ashley ran inside while I stayed outside and sat on the stoop to get some fresh air. The air was cold and rejuvenating. I couldn't figure out how tonight went from amazing to strange in a matter of seconds. I hoped Ashley would be in bed by the time I went upstairs and also that she would be in a better mood in the morning.

Ashley was still showering when I finally came upstairs. While I waited for her to finish, I made myself a peanut butter and jelly sandwich—I realized I hadn't eaten anything all night besides mozzarella sticks. It was nice to be back home in our cozy, two-bedroom apartment.

We lived on the Upper West Side, and unlike the usual skyscrapers of New York, our building was only three stories high—our apartment being one of the four units on the top floor. Our landlord, Tim, had inherited it after his father—who had lived here for several decades—passed away. He had no use for it because he lived in the suburbs with his wife and four children, so he decided to sublet it out to make a few extra bucks on the side.

It was a little farther from work than we wanted, but since it was a rent-controlled apartment, we paid next to nothing, and we weren't passing that up. It was a quiet neighborhood and only two blocks away from Central Park.

As I was finishing my sandwich, Ashley flew out of the bathroom past me and into her room. I wasn't ecstatic about how she was acting, but I was beginning to worry about her. I wondered what Nate did this time to make her so upset... Did he flat out reject her? Kiss another girl? I decided that if she was still awake when I was done showering, I would try to talk to her again.

My thoughts drifted to Mark and the kiss we shared. He was sweet and charming—nothing like Nate and the few other friends of his I had met before, who were usually just as self-centered and obnoxious as Nate was. I wondered if he was actually going to call me or if that was just him being nice.

It didn't matter anyway, I thought. Although he was nice and the kiss between us was amazing, it was just that, an amazing New Year's Eve kiss and nothing more.

I pushed all thoughts of Ashley and Mark aside for now because I was exhausted and ready to go to bed.

After my shower, I was walking back into my room when I heard Ashley's door open slowly behind me.

Riley, she said quietly.

I turned around eagerly, glad that she was at least speaking to me again, and said, "Yes?"

But as the words were coming out of my mouth, I saw her eyes widen as if she were seeing a ghost again. She hastily wiped the shocked expression from her face and walked toward me, curiosity showing in her eyes.

So, you can hear me?

"Yes, of course I can hear you, Ashley! What is going on with you? You're scaring me and quite frankly also pissing me—" I stopped as I realized her lips had never moved when she spoke.

"Wait a minute..." I said more calmly, trying to rationalize the fact that I heard her speak although no words had come out of her mouth.

Yeah, you're hearing my thoughts right now... she said—or thought—and slowly, I began to feel as if I was the one seeing a ghost.

This time when she spoke, her lips were moving. "That's what I thought! I didn't believe it earlier in the hallway. I thought you were losing your mind, then I thought maybe it was me losing my mind. I knew it was impossible, but you were literally answering my thoughts." She paused for a breath while I still stood there staring at her, open-mouthed, as she continued. "While I was in the shower I figured I would test it out one more time and well, this is nuts!"

"This can't be possible," I muttered as I sat down slowly on the couch.

Ashley sat down next to me, and I heard, *There has to be an explanation...*

"Well, of course there has to be an explanation! But this is imposs—wait, did I just do it again?"

Yes!

"Stop it! Use your words!" I yelled. "I'm freaked out enough as it is!"

"Sorry," she said with a small smirk on her face. "You have to admit though, it's kind of cool."

"Cool is not the word I was thinking." I tried to figure out how this could have happened, as this kind of stuff only happened in sci-fi movies or cheesy rom-coms. And why me? Why now? I wasn't hearing people's thoughts when the night started. Maybe I was dreaming...

"I need a drink," I said.

Then I heard, *Me too.*

I shot Ashley a sideways look. I was not going to get used to this anytime soon and hoped it would be gone by the morning.

I pulled the towel off my head and let my wet hair fall over my shoulders while Ashley poured us both a glass of wine. We were both quiet for a long time, to the point where I wondered if it had already gone away because I doubted Ashley's mind ever stopped going. I found it odd that she would have nothing to say.

I looked up at her and said, "Say something; you're being too quiet."

"I don't know what to say! Plus, you told me not to think, so I'm trying not to think! It's really hard." She paused and then asked, "Are you sure you didn't fall and hit you head or have a laced drink?" *Not that there is any kind of drug that could do this...*

"I think I'd remember falling. Plus, it was a perfectly normal night as far as I know. Mark and I kissed, but I doubt that it had anything to do with it unless his lips are radioactive." I laughed despite myself, knowing that was ridiculous.

Wait, wait, wait—what?! "You and Mark kissed?!" she asked excitedly.

"Yes. I wanted to tell you earlier, but you were acting like you were mad at me or something."

"Sorry about that... Tell me about it now! I want all the details."

"There's not much to tell. After you dropped him off—thanks for that by the way—we talked until midnight and then we kissed."

"Uh huh, and then what?" she pried. *Too much tongue? Not enough tongue? Did his breath smell bad?*

"Ashley!" I laughed.

"Oops, sorry... I already forgot you could hear that. This is going to take some time to get used to."

"Yes, it is," I answered absently. "But anyway, nothing crazy happened. I gave him my number, but I doubt he will call. Now stop stalling and tell me what happened to you tonight?"

Ugh, do I have to?

I said nothing as I stared at her, waiting for her to begin, and once she did, there was no holding her back. She started with leaving Mark and me on the balcony to go back inside and find Nate. She had been chatting with Mark and Nate inside, when Nate mentioned that she should introduce Mark to me.

"So that's when I brought him outside, thinking it was him trying to get rid of Mark so he and I could be alone, but really it was to get rid of me because when I went back inside—after taking a detour to the bar to grab a few shots of tequila—I came back and found him and Natalie making out."

She took a large sip of her wine and continued, "I stood there, looking like an idiot. I couldn't take my eyes off them. Then he pulled her into his room. I took both shots of tequila and went back to the bar."

"Oh Ash, I'm so sorry."

"No you're not, but I don't blame you, you've been trying to tell me that he's a jerk." She looked down at her almost empty glass and added, "I mean, I know I wasn't good enough for him, but Natalie? Come on! She sucks!"

"Don't even go there! Nate is not good enough for *you* and you know it. He's an ass and you deserve better."

"Yeah, yeah... Well, you can finally say it."

"Say what?" I knew what she meant but this wasn't the time to say it.

"You know what..." She looked at me through hazy, dark blue eyes.

"I don't know what you're talking about. All I will say is you can and will do better," I said. "Ugh, I hate him. What a jerk!"

"Thank you."

I hugged her and heard, *I just wish I would've kicked him in the nuts.*

"Me too."

"So, what are you going to do about..." Ashley started to ask.

"I have no idea! I have no clue how or why it started," I responded. "Hopefully I'll just sleep it off."

Right... That seems logical. Ashley muttered sarcastically to herself.

FOUR

I rolled over in bed the following morning, feeling the wrath of last night's alcohol, and saw 9:04 flashing in bright red letters on my alarm clock. My head was pounding, and I wasn't ready to get up and find out if I could still hear people's thoughts or not. I still held out hope that it was all just a dream, except for the kiss with Mark, but even that felt too good to be true.

I stayed in bed until I couldn't take the throbbing in my head anymore; I needed water and an ibuprofen. I pulled my Yale sweater on and headed for the bathroom first.

Ashley was banging around in the kitchen cooking breakfast when I came out of my room. I was always amazed by her immunity to hangovers, knowing very well that she had much more to drink last night than I did.

The smells of a fresh pot of coffee and bacon sizzling on the stove filled the air. I sat at the island, where Ashley poured me a giant cup of coffee, and I said gratefully to her, "Have I ever told you that you're my hero?"

She laughed and went back to cooking, but not before saying, *I still don't understand how you can drink your coffee like that.*

"Don't judge, I like to actually taste my coffee, not drown it in cream and sugar." Reality smacked me in the face as she stood there, spatula suspended in the air. "Crap... I was really hoping it was all a dream."

"Even the part about Mark?" She winked.

"Everything but that part!" My mouth twitched into a smile.

"If it makes you feel better, I thought I was dreaming, too," she said. "What are you going to do?"

"I don't know," I whispered. "I want to know what it means? And should I see a doctor? Am I dying or going crazy?" All of these questions were making my headache even worse.

"Don't be silly; you're not dying or going crazy," Ashley said, being the voice of reason. "I think..."

It's kind of fascinating... getting to hear what people think about you or what they are going to say before they say it... "Think of what you could do with that power!"

I didn't see the fascination of my predicament. I also didn't want to know what people were thinking of me or what they were going to say next. I drank my coffee in silence for a moment, thinking that it all seemed very strange.

She handed me a plate full of fried eggs, bacon, and toast. "Happy birthday, by the way."

"Thank you, roomie."

"What are you doing today?" she asked in between bites.

"Well, considering my new superpower, probably nothing." I wasn't thrilled at the prospect of going out in public like this, but eventually Ashley convinced me otherwise. I figured it would be better being with her than going out alone.

I headed to my room to change and stopped. "Hey, I know this goes without saying, but can we keep this between us until I figure out what the hell is going on?"

"Yes, absolutely," she said. *Your secret is safe with me.*

The phone rang, and I hurried to answer it, secretly hoping it was Mark. I was only slightly disappointed to hear my mom and dad on the other line, singing happy birthday.

"Hi Mom, hi Dad... Thank you," I said a little embarrassed.

"How was your night, sweetie?" asked my mom.

"Oh, it was—interesting—to say the least." I was usually open with my mom, but I meant it when I told Ashley I wanted to keep this between me and her for now.

"That's good. Ya'll went to that party you were telling me about?"

"Yes, only until midnight, and then we left." I told her about the view of Times Square from Nate's balcony and the ball dropping—which I made up because I missed it thanks to Mark and his lovely lips.

She told me about Barry and Judy's party they went to last night. Barry and Judy were our neighbors down the road. After my siblings and I moved out, Barry and Judy took over the task of hosting the big New Year's Eve party that my family used to throw. The parties became too much for my parents to host without us being there to help clean up the next day.

"That's great. I'm glad y'all had fun," I said absently.

"Is everything okay, Riley?"

She always knew when something was bothering me. "Yeah, Mom, I'm just tired. It was a long night. Plus, I was just getting ready to run some errands with Ashley."

"Alright, I won't keep you. I just wanted to wish you a happy birthday!" she said. After Dad added his goodbyes, Mom said, "Before I let you go, do you want me to tell you the story of the day you were born?"

I laughed, knowing it was coming. Every year on our birthdays, she offered to enlighten us with the story of our actual day of birth and the labor pains she endured.

"No thank you! I've heard the story twenty-nine times now; I think I know it by heart."

"Fine," she laughed, "Has your sister called you yet?"

"I don't think so, why?" I hadn't checked for any messages on the machine, but I doubted she would've called before nine o'clock.

"Oh, no reason!" She sounded excited and was doing a bad job at containing it.

"What's up with her?"

"I'll let her tell you," she said. "Have a wonderful day, sweetie."

We headed for the subway since Ashley needed to go downtown to pick up some last-minute travel items for her trip home next week. We couldn't take off work during the holidays due to a big project we were working on, which was when she usually went home to visit her family.

It was still early, so thankfully there weren't many people out, meaning there were less minds to read—or so I thought. That was until we actually got onto the subway.

There was a couple sitting across from us holding hands, wearing wedding rings, and smiling. Both were thinking about the other people they were secretly sleeping with on the side. Next to us was a young boy wearing a dark hoodie. He was talking to himself about the convenience store he was about to rob and how much trouble he would be in if his grandma found out.

Sitting on the opposite side of us next to the unfaithful couple was a middle-aged woman who used plastic surgery and Botox in an attempt to keep herself looking young. She had on a pound of make-up and was dressed like a young college girl. She wasn't even staring at Ashley and me, but all she was thinking about was how much nicer Ashley's body was than hers and what skin care products I was using to make my skin *glow like that.*

I felt uncomfortable hearing all their private thoughts—things they didn't want others to know. It was as if they were speaking loud and clear to me. Ashley, on the other hand, was happily reading a magazine about the latest celebrity gossip, holding an inner conversation with herself and sometimes with me.

"Can we get off at the next stop?" I whispered desperately to Ashley. "Please."

She looked up from her magazine and around the subway car before stopping at me. "That bad?"

"Very."

"This is all so strange! I don't know if I'll ever be able to get used to this!" I started once we made it back up to the street. "It was as if they were all having a conversation with me, except they weren't, and I was invading their privacy. What if I can't control this? What if I have to move out of the city, go somewhere rural where there's no people!?"

"Hey, calm down. You're not going to have to move away, and I'm sure it's very strange, but it's not like you're doing it on purpose."

She had a point... I was feeling guilty about something that I couldn't control.

"I can't even begin to understand what you're going through, but it's obviously not going away. It will take some getting used to and probably won't be easy to deal with, but try to find the good in this situation..." *If there is any good in this*, she thought. "Maybe it happened for a reason."

"Since when did you become so philosophical?" I teased.

"Maybe I got a superpower too last night... wisdom."

I snorted loudly, making two people who were passing by look my way.

After several stops around town, we made it back uptown right after lunch and stopped at a deli to grab some sandwiches. The deli was right outside of Central Park, so we made our way to a vacated park bench where we stopped to eat our lunch.

I wasn't sure how she did it, but Ashley's thoughts were fairly quiet all day.

It's so pretty here.

"I know. I love coming here just to sit and think. It doesn't matter what time of the year it is either. It's always nice," I said as I took a deep breath. "You've been quiet today, if you know what I mean."

"Really? I guess I didn't notice. I wouldn't say that I've thought about nothing at all today... I was just picturing a place that my family and I used to go to when I was younger—before my mom, you know—and it looked just like this, without the skyscrapers."

"Hmph," I uttered.

"What is it?"

"Well, I was just thinking that I didn't *hear* that thought." I sat forward on the bench after a thought occurred to me. "Were you thinking of any words? Like talking to yourself? Or just picturing an image?"

"I don't know. I guess it was just an image."

"So, I don't know when someone's thoughts are visual. I can only hear verbal thoughts," I said aloud, more to myself than to Ashley.

Can you hear this...? But not see that...?

"See what?"

"Nothing," she said, turning slightly red. "But now you've got your answer."

"Yeah..." One mystery of a thousand solved.

After a moment, I heard Ashley say to herself, *I have been wondering if there are others...*

"Others?" The possibility of others hadn't even crossed my mind, but then again I'd only had half a day to think about this, and all I could think about was what other people were thinking about.

"I mean, why not? Not that you're not special or anything, but if having a gift like this is possible, do you really think you're the only person in the world with it?"

"You have a point. I haven't really thought about it." I paused. "I'm still trying to figure out how this even happened."

"Why don't you call someone at DC Comics? Maybe ask for a job application while you're at it, too," she giggled to herself.

"Oh my gosh, stop!" I yelled at her, even though I was holding in a laugh. "I can't believe you!"

"You're right, I'm sorry." She stifled a laugh and added, "You should probably just call the X-Men directly. I'm sure they'll be looking for you."

Five

"You need time off?" Fred, my boss, slowly repeated my request back to me, one of his eyebrows raised. To anyone else, his question could have come off as mere concern, but thanks to my new power, I knew better.

While his long and worn face remained neutral, his thoughts came loud and clear. *Time off? We just had three days off! And for what? Probably was broken up with or something... She has been doing a crap job this week. Typical woman, asking for time off for a break-up—*

"Yes, please," I started, cutting his thoughts off. "I got a call over the holidays that my dad is really sick... like terminal."

I knew lying about my dad being terminal was wrong, but I felt no remorse in this case. I had been working for Fred for over two years now and had considered him, before this week, one of the kindest and most generous bosses I'd ever worked with. Now I knew it was all just an act, and a really good act at that. Fred was a miserable person who hated everything and everyone around him, including his wife and kids.

Doubt it, he mumbled internally before saying, "Oh, I'm so sorry to hear that. I will keep him in my prayers."

"Thank you," I said politely with a smile, knowing damn well he wasn't going to be praying for my fake-sick father. "I think it will be alright; I just need to go home and be with my family for a little while..."

What the hell is a little while?

"Maybe a week or two," I added casually.

"A week or two?" he said evenly as his eyes drifted back to the pile of papers in front of him. Besides his fist clenching, he looked like he was trying to continue the work that I'd interrupted moments ago. *A week or two?! Is she joking? With all these deadlines and the board of directors on my ass about the company tanking! If only I could fire the little—*

I cut him off once again before he could finish that lovely thought. "My team is ahead on all our projects and campaigns. We also have a final meeting scheduled with the airline in a month, which I will be back in plenty of time to prepare for. I'll brief Tyler and stay in touch with him while I'm gone to make sure we're staying on top of everything."

"Sounds like you've got it under control," he said with a smile. *It's not like I can tell her no.* "We're here if you need anything. Take all the time you need."

As I closed the door to Fred's office, I gave Ashley a thumbs up to signal that we were good to go.

This week had been anything but normal, and I hadn't learned anything new about my power except that I couldn't hear anyone's thoughts if they were over ten feet away from me.

Last night, Ashley suggested that I take some time off to look for answers—not that I knew where to even begin—but I decided to start by going home. She was leaving in the morning to visit her family in Ohio for a week, so I offered to drive her there and make the rest of the drive home to Texas by myself.

"Ashley, I'll meet you downstairs... I need to talk with Tyler before I go," I said as everyone was packing up to leave at the end of the day. "Tyler, can you come in my office for a minute please?"

"Sure thing boss!" Tyler put his bag down that he had just slung over his shoulder and headed into my office.

Tyler was a nice guy who became my assistant manager last summer right out of grad school. He was a favorite with all the ladies in the office, commonly being referred to behind his back as a Brad Pitt look-a-like. Not that he cared or even noticed. He only cared about doing well at work. He was a great assistant and one of the only people's thoughts I could stand to be around all week.

I felt better about leaving for a few weeks with Tyler around. As he jotted down all my instructions, he remained calm and professional. On the inside, he was thrilled about taking on more responsibility to prove himself worthy of a promotion. I was doing my best not to laugh out loud.

Once we were back at the apartment, I started packing a bag and helped Ashley load all her bags and Christmas gifts for her family into my Jeep.

I hope this ancient piece of crap doesn't give us any trouble tomorrow.

"Hey! You do remember that I can hear that, right?" I said.

"Yes, I know. I meant what I said."

"She will be fine... This ol' girl and me have been on a lot of road trips. Plus she's not even that old!" I rebutted.

"Yeah, but you haven't driven it in months."

I wasn't going to admit that she had a point, but so far my Jeep hadn't let me down.

"We will be fine," I said overly confident. "Come on, I want to get to bed."

Even knowing that we had to get up and drive all day long in a few hours, I couldn't sleep. I didn't know what to expect of this trip. I didn't even really believe that there were any answers to be found, especially not in Texas. All I knew was that I needed to start somewhere. I decided not to call my parents, thinking a surprise visit would be better than them wondering why I was coming home all of a sudden, considering I hadn't been home since last Christmas.

I finally dozed off and felt as if I had only been asleep for five minutes when I woke to Ashley knocking on my door at five in the morning. It was about a ten-hour drive from New York to Ohio. We had taken this same trip once before when we first moved in together. She usually flew when she went home, except for the last time we did this drive—which she stated would be the last time she was stuck in a car that long. But she had so much stuff to bring home this time that she was planning to rent a car there and then fly back in a week. I always drove when I went home, not minding the long hours on the road alone.

"Are we there yet?" Ashley jokingly groaned after being on the road for only an hour.

"Not even close."

This part of the drive was all interstate through small mountain towns and vast farmlands. Thankfully, it wasn't snowing anywhere, but there was still ice on the ground in some areas. We stopped to swap places and to eat an early lunch in Bedford, Pennsylvania, a quaint little river town mid-way through our journey.

"So, do you have any idea where you're going to start looking?" Ashley started once we were back on the road.

"I have no clue," I said, gazing out the window.

I still think there are others out there.

"Even if that's true, I wouldn't even know how to find them."

True.

I didn't answer her, but after a moment I looked at her and said, "What would you do?"

"I honestly don't know," she said. "I've been thinking about that, and I feel like there's got to be somebody you can talk to, or a book about this somewhere, right? But then I've thought, if there are more people that this happened to the same night as you, surely we'd know about them by now. Then again, maybe not because they're scared of being deemed a freak."

"Thanks." I gave her a sideways look.

"You know what I mean," she laughed.

"Yeah, I do." We said nothing more about it.

When we finally arrived at her dad's house, he and his girlfriend, Pamela, came outside to greet us and help unload our stuff.

"Hey girls, how was the drive?" Ricky, her dad, asked as he hugged Ashley.

"Hey Dad," she said, hugging him back. "It was a long, uneventful drive but good."

"You still have quite a way to go, huh Riley?" Ricky asked me as he grabbed our bags from the back. *And in this hunk of junk?* he thought.

"Yes sir, roughly eighteen hours, but I've done it plenty of times before," I said.

"She's going to sleep here tonight and leave early in the morning, if that's alright," Ashley interjected.

"Of course she's welcome to stay here," Pamela, who according to Ashley was a dimwit, said in a bubbly tone. "I've made plenty of lasagna for dinner."

At the same time, Ricky and Ashley's thoughts mimicked one another. *Oh great,* insinuating that her lasagna was not great.

"Mmm, sounds delicious," Ashley said, trying her best to be nice. "Where's Allen?"

Allen was Ashley's twin brother. Ashley believed that Allen felt like she abandoned him when she moved to Manhattan because he never returned her phone calls, nor did he show any interest in ever visiting her. She thought to herself on the drive over here how excited she was to see him because they hadn't spoken in over three years.

"He doesn't get off work until midnight these days," Ricky said as he led the way inside.

Ashley and I were able to both clean up before dinner, which I now understood the lack of excitement over. Pamela's lasagna was not the worst meal I'd ever eaten, but it was definitely better than the gas station junk food we'd been eating all day.

"This lasagna is great, Ms. Pamela," I said politely.

Oh my gosh, are you kidding? Ashley thought directly to me.

"Oh, please honey, call me Pam," she said. Then she added while batting her long fake eyelashes at Ashley's dad, "And thank you. It's Ricky's favorite."

He smiled through his thick mustache, nodded his head slightly, and took a long sip of his beer. *I'm going to have to pay for cooking classes for this woman one of these days. I don't know how much longer I can take undercooked noodles.*

I helped Ashley with the dishes after dinner and then watched as she poured us both another glass of wine before heading into the living room where Ricky and Pam were sitting.

The living room was small and dark. Most of the decor was unchanged from when Ashley's mom was still alive. Ashley's dad was a simple person who didn't like change. It had been almost two years since the last time I saw him, and I would've bet my last paycheck that he was wearing the same red flannel shirt and worn out faded blue jeans as the last time. The only difference I noticed in him were a few more gray hairs in his sideburns and mustache.

Pam also wasn't as big of a dimwit as Ashley liked to make her out to be. She owned a local hair salon and apparently used to cut the entire family's hair before Ashley's mom passed away. After that, she'd come over to help Ricky with Ashley and her brother, and she hadn't left Ricky's side since then. I could tell that he enjoyed her companionship and cared about her, but everyone, including Pam, knew she'd never be number one in any of their lives.

I sat there quietly, enjoying their conversation about Ashley's life in New York and the small-town dramas that she had missed out on back home. I only needed to answer the occasional question. The fatigue from being on the road all day, eating a heavy meal at dinner, and two glasses of wine was spreading through my veins quickly. I excused myself shortly after finishing my glass, knowing I had another long day ahead of me tomorrow.

Ashley jumped up to tell me goodbye since I'd be gone before she woke up in the morning. She hugged me and said quietly, "Be careful tomorrow, and call me when you make it home." And added, *I hope you find some answers.*

"Yes, ma'am," I said as I hugged her back. Then I whispered, "Me too."

Before getting into bed, I used Ashley's pink princess phone on her bedside table to check our messages back at the apartment, just in case Tyler or my mom had called.

There was only one message on our machine, and to my surprise, it was from Mark.

"Hey Riley, I am sorry to call so late, but I wanted to see if you had any plans tonight. Thought you might want to grab a drink. Give me a call. 555-1324. Bye."

I hung up the phone and burrowed under the covers. I thought I should've been more bothered that it took him almost a week to call after our kiss on New Year's Eve, but I'd been so distracted with my new superpower—that's what Ashley had been calling it all week—that I'd actually forgotten about giving him my number. I also felt as if I should've been more excited that he called at all, but I wasn't. It was better off that way anyway. I couldn't date anyone right now.

I fell asleep within minutes, exhaustion spreading through me like wildfire. I dreamt of nothing at first. Then, what felt like only minutes later, but was actually hours, I woke up to the loud sound of wind rushing through Ashley's room. It was as if a window blew open from a thunderstorm. I thought I was dreaming but realized that I was wide awake and staring into the eyes of a girl standing over me. She had a bright golden-white glow around her, allowing me to make out the details of her features. She was pretty but plain looking and seemed to be the same age as me. The girl had long, straight brown hair with matching brown eyes.

I knew I couldn't still be dreaming and wondered if Ashley was awake and staring into the same face.

Before I could turn my head to see, she said loud and clear,

Joanna Glasglow is no longer with us.
The ability has passed on to Tracey Finley.

Then she vanished as quickly as she appeared.

Six

I sat up quickly and turned around to see Ashley's reaction
to the ghostly appearance. Instead, I found her fast asleep,
breathing steadily under the covers, with her back facing me.
I looked around the room, half expecting the girl to still be
there somewhere in the darkness or the window to be open,
but there was nothing except the glow of the moonlight
outside the closed window.

Ashley's desk clock flashed 2:07 a.m. in red digits, so I laid
back down and tried to fall asleep again, hoping for just a
few more hours of sleep before getting back on the road. It
was hopeless though. The mystery of the dream—if it was a
dream—loomed over me. What was it? Or better yet, *who* was
it? I didn't know anyone named Joanna or Tracey.

It was obvious that this was connected to me hearing
people's thoughts—she said *ability*, which sounded better
than superpower—but how?

After several long minutes, I knew I wasn't going back to
sleep.

Within the next hour I was dressed and back on the
road, the image of the girl standing over me still fresh in
my mind. There weren't many cars on the road this early in
the morning, and for the first time in a week, I felt alone.
Alone with my thoughts and no one else's, I began to feel
that I needed solidarity more than I needed to find answers
at home.

Being alone with my thoughts, though, meant all the questions I'd been avoiding asking myself came flooding at once.

Why am I reading minds?

Is there anyone else? If so, how do I find them?

Who was that girl? Why did she appear to me?

Was she Joanna? And why was she gone now?

Were Mark's lips really radioactive?

After the last question crossed my mind, I turned up the volume on the radio, hoping to drown it all out before I really lost my mind. I had an outlandish thought that maybe I could find something at the library about this. I just had to figure out what section *Why am I hearing people's thoughts?* was under.

I passed through Indianapolis as the sun began to rise and stopped for gas and coffee on the outskirts of town. I noticed that there were several mounds of snow on the ground nearby and along the sides of the road, the chill in the air keeping the snow from melting.

The drive between Indianapolis and Oklahoma was my favorite part of trip. Living in a big city like Manhattan was magical with the towering skyscrapers and endless amounts of places to eat, shop, and peruse, but there was something about driving along the countryside from the flat farmlands to the rocky, picturesque landscapes, most of it untouched and undeveloped.

The hours rolled on as I made my way further south. It was mesmerizing to see the topography change so drastically from state to state and even city to city. I imagined what it would have been like hundreds of years ago when people travelled over the same lands with no maps or roads to guide them. Using only the elements provided by nature, they navigated this uncharted land in order to survive.

I came up with ten more unanswerable questions by the time I reached Oklahoma City. A bright orange flashing sign advised there was major construction on my normal route through Dallas, so I took I-40 toward Amarillo, hoping to save some time.

I was an hour and a half past Oklahoma City when I noticed I had less than a quarter tank of gas, and my eyes were beginning to feel heavy. My hope of arriving home that evening was quickly shattered.

"It wouldn't be the worst thing to stop somewhere for the night and finish the drive early in the morning," I said aloud to myself, as if I were convincing someone else in the car as to why I should stop.

A fluorescent green exit sign up ahead read "ARKDALE / LOGAN – 2 MILES," and another blue sign shortly after that one advertised at least one gas station at this exit.

"Hopefully someone there can recommend a good place to sleep," I said, once again talking to the non-existent person in the car with me.

On the exit ramp, another sign pointed to the right for the gas station and Logan, twelve miles up the road; a left arrow indicated that Arkdale was eighteen miles to the south. As expected, a few miles up the road was a small mom and pop Conoco station, which looked deserted except for the flashing neon sign on the front window suggesting otherwise.

I left the pump running on my Jeep while I went inside, where I could hear an elderly woman rattling off her to-do list internally as I walked through the door.

Finish stocking the candy bars. Take out the trash. Wipe the counters. Check the drink racks. Organize and restock—customer!

A short, stout woman came waddling around the corner, wearing a black checkered apron over a yellow sundress that fell to her ankles. She wore wide, low-heeled shoes, and her silver hair was pinned up neatly with a pen sticking out at the top, reminding me of Aunt Bee from *The Andy Griffith Show*.

"Hello there! How can I help you?" she said enthusiastically, followed unknowingly by, *Ooh poor darlin' looks tired. Just look at those dark circles under her eyes! I wonder what she's doing way out here. Definitely not from around here with those—*

"Hi," I offered quickly with a smile. "I'm just passing through and wondered if you could tell me if there is somewhere nearby where I can stay for the night?"

"Oh yes dear, right up the road is the cutest little inn called the Black Horse Inn," she continued without taking a breath. "If you keep heading north for a few more miles, you'll hit our little town square—that's Logan—it's a historic town, yes it is, been around since the 1800s! I've lived here my whole life, and my daddy opened this gas station and ran it himself, and then my brother and now me. They're both gone now—such great men they were—but I do my best to keep it running. My name is Maybell, but you can call me Maw Maw May."

"Oh, that's great, and thank you." I started backing toward the door and added reluctantly, "So the Black Horse Inn? It's in town?"

I didn't want to seem rude, but hunger and exhaustion were weighing on me like a ton of bricks.

"Yes, honey." *Look at me just blabbering on,* she thought. "Like I said, keep heading north when you leave here, and once you get to Logan—you can't miss it, the road ends right at the town square—take a right onto South Street at the welcome sign. That road will turn into Black Horse Way at the east intersection... but don't turn on East Street! Or else you'll be goin' the wrong way! Just stay to the right and you'll be fine... you'll know you're goin' the right way when you see a little white church on your left." *Although she may not be able to see that in the dark.* "Go about a quarter of a mile and that'll take you right to the Black Horse Inn. If you see a big red barn you've gone too far!"

I had one foot out the door as she finished and said, "Thank you so much, Ms. May, I really appreciate it."

Now I told her to call me Maw Maw May. What is it with these city folk? "No problem at all honey, you come back if you need anything!" She smiled and waved.

"Yes ma'am, have a nice night." With that, I slid the rest of my body out the door. I laughed to myself as I turned the ignition, thinking of small-town people like Maybell back home, who were overly welcoming to all newcomers.

I followed her directions and easily found my way to the town. Although it was getting too dark to see all my surroundings, Logan looked like a charming town. The town square at the end of the road wasn't hard to miss as it was brightly lit and looked more like a small park that the town was built around on purpose. There were walkways crossing through the square and benches placed evenly along the paths, reminding me of a mini Central Park. I noticed that there weren't many people walking around, but it was still early.

I followed the winding roads per Maybell's instructions and turned right at a white and black wood sign indicating my arrival at the Black Horse Inn. The road was surrounded by a dark silhouette of trees on either side, the moon's reflection on the gravel road being the only source of light leading the way. I wondered for a moment if I'd taken a wrong turn when the inn revealed itself after the second bend in the road.

My first impression of the two-story, ranch style house was that it belonged on the front of a postcard. Even in the dark of night, it was picturesque with Christmas lights hanging from every eave, tree, and bush surrounding the building, which reflected off a large pond that now followed alongside the road. I coasted up the driveway slowly, taking it all in, noticing that the lights extended along a walkway leading to a small gravel parking lot to the left of the property. Similar lights also followed a path into the woods beyond the pond to the right, and I wondered if that was a path leading back to the town square.

I parked in the lot, empty except for one other car, and grabbed my bag from the back of the Jeep. As I headed for the entrance, I saw several gas lanterns lighting the white-washed walls of the wrap around porch and bouncing rays of yellow light off the dark, navy colored shutters along each window.

When I walked through the French doors, I was welcomed by a roaring fire in a small den to the left, where four vacant sitting chairs rested. Directly in front of me was a staircase, presumably leading up to the rooms of the inn.

To my right was a small room with an old oak receptionist desk. Behind it sat a younger guy whose head was buried in a car magazine. He looked up as I approached and thought, *A customer? Damn it! Trudy said there shouldn't be any customers until the middle of the week. I was hoping for a chill night.*

Still, he put the biggest, most fake smile on his face and said, "Hello! Welcome to the Black Horse Inn. How can I help you?"

He couldn't have been more than nineteen years old based on his adolescent chin stubble and a few pimples showing on his pale cheeks. His face was thin, like the brown hair on his head, which hung down to his eyebrows. The small, green nametag on his shirt indicated his name was Kyle.

I returned Kyle's fake smile and said, "Hi, I am just passing through for the night and was told by a Ms. Maybell that this was the best place to stay."

Oh, gee thanks Maw Maw May... kooky old lady. Well, at least it's only one night.

"She told you correctly! Best place in town and I'll make sure you get our best room," Kyle said cheerily, and then, *Joke's on you, all the rooms are the same. But Trudy insists on making everyone feel special.*

"Thank you." I hid a smile to myself by looking around at the room while he checked me in.

I had to hand it to him that his customer service skills, though they were fake, were excellent. After checking me in quickly, he showed me to my room up the stairs and even surprised me when he offered to carry my bag.

My room proved to be just as charming as the rest of the place. It had one queen sized bed, a large antique chest of drawers in the opposite corner, and a vanity table and chair on the same wall as the small adjoining bathroom. The theme of this room was colonial blue, a decoration I was remarkably familiar with due to my mother's love of antiques and all things colonial style.

I settled in and showered before calling Ashley to let her know I'd stopped for the night. Then, I fought the urge to climb in the bed even though it was only half past seven. My stomach growled though, so I headed out in search of food.

Kyle told me to follow the walking path I saw earlier leading into the woods—which did in fact go back to town—where there were several places to eat since the kitchen at the inn was closed for the night.

My skepticism of walking along a path through the woods in a strange town must have shown on my face because he thought, *Is she worried about being taken or something? Nothing exciting ever happens in this boring town.*

"Don't worry, it's a really well-lit path, and I don't think a crime has been committed here in over a hundred years."

Against my normal judgement and due to my need for food, I figured if his thoughts didn't allude to danger, then I was okay. Plus, at least one person knew where I was if I did go missing.

Seven

Kyle was telling the truth. The path—a wide, smooth gravel trail—was well-lit by cast iron light poles placed twenty feet apart from one another. Though there was decent lighting on the path, I was not able to see further than a few feet off the edges of the path. It was quiet, peaceful even, and I could feel a cool breeze blowing through the dense silhouette of trees on both sides of me. My tension about potentially being followed began to subside, so much so that I eased up on my grip of the small black pocketknife I carried with me just in case.

After fifteen minutes, the trail ended across the street from the town square. Still a ghost town, I did see several more people than there were earlier walking around as I crossed the street. I followed the sidewalk that ran directly through the middle of the square, toward the opposite side of the square, where it looked most promising to find a restaurant.

Bordering the other two sides of the square were all sorts of small, local shops—Katie's Pet Store, The Barber Shop, Joe's Ice Cream Shop, Logan Grocery and Deli, The Burger Hut, and several others whose signs were too small to read.

The town, like the inn, still had their Christmas decorations on display in all the trees, bushes, windows, and along the tops of the buildings, giving it a feeling of needing to be on the back of a postcard, like the inn.

I finally approached what looked like the only open restaurant at the moment. There was a wood plaque hanging over the door with the word "BLACKY'S" carved in dark, bold letters. The outside brick of the building was also painted black to match the lettering in the sign, but the door and window frames were a dark hunter green, worn from years of use.

My mouth watered as the greasy smells from inside emitted through the door that was propped open with a brick.

This could easily have been the oldest building in town. While clean, I felt as if I'd stepped onto an old pirate ship. The floor, walls, and ceiling beams were constructed of the same darkly stained wood planks that I saw once at a marauder's museum. The place was modest in size but had several wooden circular tables big enough to accommodate larger parties, while several square shaped tables sat along the walls on either side for smaller parties.

Besides the yellow tea lights flickering at each table and the sconce bulbs placed above each of the square tables, the only other light offered was from the kitchen through a rectangular pass-through window behind the bar along the back wall.

There were several tables occupied, but I walked toward the bar where two older men sat. The bar ran almost the entire length of the back of the room before it stopped short next to a hallway, which I assumed led to the kitchen or the back of the building.

The two men were sitting at the end next to the hallway, focusing on a dinky TV sitting behind the bar. I took a seat at the opposite end to avoid hearing anyone's thoughts. Unfortunately, as I passed them on my way to the barstool, I still heard, *I thought the tourists weren't supposed to be arriving until the middle of the week,* and, *Never seen that pretty little thing around here before... Wonder where she blew in from?*

There hadn't been anyone behind the bar since I walked in, but I spotted a paper menu sitting on the countertop next to me and perused it while I waited for someone to come back.

The men refocused their attention on their fuzzy television when a short woman with short spiky hair and a nose ring came out of the hallway carrying a tray of food. She set the food down in front of the two old men, smiled, and grabbed each of them two more beers without asking before noticing me at the other end of the bar.

I hope she hasn't been waiting too long, I heard as she got closer to me before she said, "Hey there, what can I get for you?"

"Hi, a Bud Light and the Blacky Burger with fries, please," I answered, desperate for food.

"Dressed?"

"Yes, please... and thank you."

"Coming right up," she said before disappearing into the hallway again.

She reappeared as quickly as she'd gone, grabbed my beer from a deep cooler behind the bar, popped the top off from a bottle opener she had sticking out of her jean shorts pocket, and placed it in front of me.

"I take it you're not from around here," she said as she leaned up against the bar and crossed her arms, which were both heavily covered with a tapestry of delicately placed tattoos from shoulder to wrist, most of the artwork consisting of animal portraits and horoscopic symbols.

"No, I'm just passing through on my way to Lubbock."

"Lubbock? Nice place, I've been there once or twice." She smiled as she quickly glanced around the restaurant to make sure none of her patrons needed anything, then added, "Where are you coming from?"

I swallowed a mouthful of my beer before answering, "New York. I'm heading down to visit my parents. They live just outside the city."

Holy crap, she drove from New York! "Holy crap! You drove from New York? That's a pretty long drive isn't it?"

"Yes, it is," I laughed.

"I've never been but I've always heard that it's a neat place to visit."

"Yeah, I love living there. Quite different from being in a small town like this, that's for sure," I said. "Don't get me wrong, I miss the small-town life sometimes, but I love my job and the people in the city."

She smiled politely but instead of responding, she thought, *You couldn't pay me enough money to go back to a big city like that, but to each their own.*

"It's not for everyone though," I added. "How was it growing up around here?"

"Oh, I'm not from around here. I'm from Chicago, but I've lived here just over ten years now." *Why did you say Chicago? She's not one of Frankie's informants... that was a long time ago, Staci.*

"Chicago's nice! How did you end up here?" She couldn't have been much older than me. Aside from the dark circles under her eyes, her face didn't have any signs of aging yet.

"Oh, ya know, I was just looking for a fresh start, drove all over wanting to get away from the city. One day, I broke down here and never left." The corner of her mouth twitched, and I heard, *Just your run-of-the-mill runaway story.* After a moment, she added, "You said you loved your job. What do you do?"

"I manage my own marketing consultation team. We work with all kinds of companies in the city, advising them on the best marketing strategies to grow their business, and we also manage their advertising."

Sounds boring. "Sounds interesting!" she replied.

I laughed a little to myself behind my beer. "It's not my dream job, but I've met some great people doing it. It's also rewarding, whether I am collaborating with a large corporation or helping a small business grow. Plus it pays the bills."

"I can appreciate that."

At the same time, a squirrely kitchen cook placed my burger on the window behind her and repeatedly dinged a small call bell with a mischievous smile on his face.

She rolled her eyes as she turned around. *For Christ's sake Pauly, I'm right here!*

Scowling at him she said, "Thank you, Pauly." She took the plate and placed it in front of me. "Here ya go. I've got to go check on a few people in the back but let me know if you need anything else. By the way, my name is Staci."

"I will. Thank you Staci."

I ate my burger in silence, except for the two older men arguing over the turnout of the game they were watching on the TV and the rising volume of conversations in the restaurant as people began filing in to eat. Staci ran back and forth making drinks and grabbing food, checking on me occasionally.

After the dinner rush settled, Staci came over and leaned against the bar near me once again.

"I'm curious," she started, "how *did* you end up here off the interstate? There's not many signs for Logan out there."

"I was running low on gas, and this was the next exit that looked promising. I also knew I wasn't going to make it all the way home, so I was hoping there would be somewhere to stay for the night. I stopped at the Conoco—"

Oh Maw Maw May...

"—where a Ms. Maybell told me there was no better place than the Black Horse Inn. And here I am," I explained.

"Maw Maw May," she said. "She's a sweet old woman but a little on the kooky side. She's always trying to get more people to visit Logan. I'm sure she told you she's been living here her whole life."

We both laughed and I said, "Yes she did. I'm grateful though because there's not much on this stretch of interstate, and I've been driving since two a.m., so needless to say it was time for a break."

Holy shit, she's nuts! "Holy shit, you're nuts! How are you still awake and functioning?"

"Barely."

Staci was in the middle of a story about the first time she met Maybell when a man—who was tall and brawny, with a short trimmed, dark beard—stepped out of the hallway on the side of the bar making his way toward Staci.

"Hey Staci, I gave Timmy and Jayden a bottle of champagne on the house."

Ha! I heard before she said it aloud. "Ha! I knew they would sucker you into a free bottle too if you showed up here tonight!"

"How many have they had?" the man asked, amused and unfazed that he'd just been tricked into giving someone a free bottle of champagne.

"Well, let's see," Staci began, counting on her fingers. "I gave them their first complementary bottle when they got here, and Moe bought them a second one about an hour ago." She gestured toward one of the men sitting at the other end of the bar. "Making yours the third one of the night."

She laughed and he just smiled and shrugged his shoulders.

"Can you blame them?" he asked as he glanced my way, noticing my presence for the first time since he entered the bar. "They deserve to celebrate."

"They absolutely do! But don't worry, I offered to drive them home when they were ready," Staci added.

Staci, noticing that he was looking my way, turned her attention back to me to introduce us to one another. "Oh, Ben this is—well actually, I'm sorry, I never got your name."

"That's alright, it's Riley. Riley Bandoni."

"Riley, this is Ben. He owns Blacky's and pretty much every other business in town."

"Don't listen to her. I don't own every other business in town. Nice to meet you though," he said, smiling politely. He continued to look my way, and I noticed his expression changed slightly, as if he recognized me from somewhere.

My attention turned back toward Staci as she explained what—and who—they were talking about previously, feeling Ben's eyes on me all the while.

"We have these kids sitting on the back patio celebrating their long-awaited engagement—the town has basically raised both of them. They've been together since they were teenagers, and Tim finally proposed to her today on their ten-year anniversary. Total sweethearts and the nicest kids you'll ever meet. They deserve some happiness," she said, then lowered her voice slightly. "They've had a pretty tough childhood, both of them."

"Aww, well good for them," I said sincerely. "I'd offer to buy them a drink, but it seems like they've had enough."

"You've got that right!" Staci said.

Ben, who was still standing there, asked me, "Riley, where are you coming from?"

Staci answered for me before I could. "New York!"

"Whoa, that's quite a hike. What brings you out this way?" he asked, looking from her back to me.

"Yeah. I'm just passing through on my way home to Lubbock."

Two people walked in, sat down at a table by the window, and shouted at Staci to bring some menus. Both her and Ben looked at each other, and she sauntered off to the couple, leaving Ben and me alone.

"So, you own the whole town, huh?" I asked him when I finished my beer.

"No, I don't," he said smiling. "I'm sorry, but what did you say your name was again?"

"Riley Bandoni."

"That's right. Well, it was nice to meet you, Riley. I've got to go, but let us know if you need anything, alright?"

"Will do. Thank you, Ben."

I asked Staci for the bill when she came back from the rowdy couple at the front table.

"I don't know how quick you're trying to get out of here in the morning, but the diner on the corner has some of the best coffee and eggs benedict around," Staci offered as I was getting up from the barstool.

"I'm not in a huge rush... my parents don't even know I'm coming home."

Staci laughed when I shrugged my shoulders, and I continued, "I'll have to swing by and check it out. If I don't see you, it was nice meeting you."

"Yeah, you too. Safe travels!" she said.

EIGHT

Once I was back in my room at the inn, I kicked off my shoes and lay on the bed, expecting sleep to come. Instead, I laid there, wide awake and buzzing from the beer and a lack of sleep.

My thoughts drifted to the handsome stranger named Ben. There was something about him that seemed familiar and mysterious. It also occurred to me, while I was remembering his dark eyes gazing at me, that the entire time he was talking with us at the bar, I never heard him utter a single thought. Which wasn't completely odd. Since having this ability, I'd come across other people whose thoughts were visual—thoughts I couldn't see or hear—but they still typically had at least one or two verbal thoughts that I could hear. There was nothing from Ben whatsoever.

I tried to forget about it as I most likely would never see him again.

For a moment, I considered calling Mark back, but I was still unsure whether I wanted to open that door. For one, he was out of my league. I couldn't understand why he was interested in me at all. On top of that, I didn't want to hear the thoughts of someone I was dating—that only seemed disastrous.

Against my better judgement, I called Mark, dialing the number he'd left on my answering machine before I even realized what I was doing.

"Hello," came the deep voice on the other end of the line.

"Hi, Mark—it's Riley," I said bashfully.

"Riley? Hey! How are you?"

"Oh, just livin' the dream." I put my hand to my face instantly, regretting saying that. "How are you?"

"Better now that you called," he said with a small huff of laughter, and I was grateful that he said something even more lame than I did.

"Does that line work for you on all the ladies?"

"Sometimes," he answered matter-of-fact.

"Poor girls."

I heard him laugh a little louder and smiled, picturing the small dimple in his cheek.

"I guess this isn't one of those times," he said.

"We will see," I answered. "I will say that I was surprised you called."

"Why is that surprising? You gave me your phone number, didn't you?"

"You know what I mean."

"Not really. I enjoyed talking with you on New Year's Eve," he said coolly and added, "It's hard to find a beautiful girl that can hold a conversation these days."

I was thankful that he couldn't see me blushing.

Before I could answer though, he said, "I know the weekend is over, but is it too late to go grab that drink?"

"I'd love to but..." I hesitated, "I'm in Oklahoma right now."

"Oh," he sounded confused.

"I had some family stuff come up last minute and started driving down here yesterday with Ashley." I explained that I had dropped her off in Ohio and told him about the rest of my trip.

"Got it. I hope everything is alright with your family."

I felt awful for lying, but there was no way I was revealing the real reason for my spontaneous trip home, so I answered,

"Oh, it's all good. I just felt that I needed to come home for a few days."

"That must be a very boring drive by yourself."

"It's not that bad," I said casually. "I've done it once or twice before since moving to New York. It's nice to drive on the open road through the countryside without a single skyscraper in sight."

"Isn't there a country song about that?"

I snorted, thinking one, that there were a million country songs about driving down some country road and two, that he knew one of them.

In my best Texas accent, I said goofily, "It ain't a real country song if it don't have a line about drivin' down a backroad."

To my relief, he laughed aloud and responded, "Is that so, Texas?"

"Texas? Seriously?"

"It suits you," he said.

"Have you ever even been to Texas? Or anywhere south of New York at all, for that matter?"

"As a matter-of-fact, I have," he responded confidently. "I've been to Texas and many other places down yonder—as your people would say."

This time I laughed. "What brought you down here? Surely not a pasture party or a rodeo."

"I'll admit that I haven't been to a rodeo, and I'm not sure what a pasture party is, but you'll have to explain that to me one day."

The phrase *one day* made butterflies dance in my stomach.

He continued, "However, I went to San Antonio once for a guy's trip, and I've been to Dallas a few times with my father on business trips."

"Okay," I conceded, "so was it on one of these trips that you learned the country song? And were you driving down a backroad when you heard it?"

He chuckled. "No, we always stayed in the city, but I can't remember... I just know it was a catchy little tune that I heard in a restaurant. Something about wide open spaces."

I started shaking with laughter, knowing exactly which song he was referring to while he was still trying to figure it out.

"Why can't I remember? It was stuck in my head for days!" He seemed to notice me laughing and asked, "Do you know the song I'm talking about?"

"Was it sung by women?"

"Yes! So you do know it?!" he exclaimed.

"Of course I know it." I couldn't contain my laughter anymore, but he didn't seem to mind. "Every girl in her twenties knows that song."

"Hey, I'm not ashamed! It's a great song." Then, in a girly voice, Mark began to sing what few words he remembered. "*Wiiiiide open spaaaces*, something, something, *make big mistakes!*"

"Wow, I think you'd make a great addition to the band—The Dixie Chicks featuring Mark."

"That's the dream."

We were still giggling when I realized how easy it was to talk to him—he was funny, confident, smart, and sweet—and what was worse, how much I enjoyed it. Another part of me was telling myself to get over it, because this couldn't become anything more than this.

I unintentionally let out a yawn, exhaustion finally taking over.

"I'm sure you're exhausted, so I can let you go if need be."

"Yeah, I'm sorry. It's been a long day, and I have more driving to do in the morning."

"Will you let me know when you're back in town?" he asked.

"Of course."

"Goodnight, Texas."

"Goodnight, Mark."

The next morning, I ventured out onto the trail early so I could see the town in the daytime.

Earlier when I had entered the lobby, Trudy, the manager—I assumed from her cheery disposition, quite the opposite of Kyle—greeted me and asked if everything in my room was alright last night.

Before I could respond I heard, *I hope Kyle didn't give her too much trouble last night. That little hoodlum can be so crude.*

"Everything was great! Thank you."

"Wonderful! I hope you'll come back to see us soon."

I decided to walk the trail again instead of driving because there was a refreshing chilly breeze blowing through the trees. It was just as peaceful as last night, especially given that no one else was out here. Halfway along the path, I stopped on the bridge that I had crossed the night before. I hadn't been able to see the surroundings in the darkness of the night.

This time, the sight was breathtaking. Trees were cascading over a small creek that flowed through boulders of assorted sizes, placed strategically by nature through the small stream. The sound of the water rushing made me forget about my predicament for a moment, and I wished I could've stayed there all day.

Eventually, I continued walking along the path and made my way to the diner that Staci had recommended. Since it was still early in the morning, the small diner was bustling with locals grabbing their coffee and breakfast before work or school. I found my way to an open seat at the white, lacquered counter, one seat away from an older gentleman who was reading today's paper and sipping on a glass of orange juice.

The waitress came up and took my order for a cup of coffee and the eggs benedict. After pouring my cup, she walked away to serve another customer who had just walked in, leaving me to take in all the noises around me. Over the last week, I had been trying to figure out a way to turn off the mind reading, or at the very least, turn it down.

I started regrettably with the old man next to me. Innocent though he seemed reading his paper, he was having some risqué thoughts of a woman who lived in his retirement community. In order to ignore *those* thoughts, I shifted my focus to a mom and her two children sitting at a small table behind me. I'd learned that children's thoughts were much more pleasant to listen to if I had a choice. The mom was rattling off her to-do list for the day, while the little boy, who looked about seven years old, was thinking of what games he and his friends could play at recess today; right now it was between pirates or knights guarding a castle.

I became entranced with the little girl's thoughts. She couldn't have been older than four or five. She was determined to master her shapes on the paper in front of her.

Circle goes around in a loop... There! And a square has four lines, that go one... two... three... and four! Perfect!

I was so engaged in the innocent thoughts of the little girl that I barely noticed that someone had sat down on the stool next to me until I heard a familiar voice say, "Good morning, Riley."

I turned to see Ben looking down at me from the seat next to me, half of his mouth curved into a smile, the beard showing more glints of red than I noticed last night. He also seemed much bigger sitting next to me than he did standing behind the bar. For reasons unknown to me, my heart was racing, and I sat there speechless.

He asked before I could form words, "How was your stay at the inn last night?"

"It was fine. Everyone there has been really friendly," I finally said.

He lifted his hand to the waitress as she passed by. Without saying a word, she flashed him a flirtatious smile, which he didn't seem to notice, and poured him a cup of coffee and walked away.

"Staci told me you might stop by here before leaving." It was more a statement than a question.

"Yes, I thought I'd check out the best coffee and eggs benedict around."

He smiled but didn't say anything for a moment, as if he was debating how to ask a certain question.

"I don't know when you're supposed to be passing back through here, but we have this big festival coming up this weekend..." he finally offered. "Everyone calls it The Post-Winter Festival because they're all celebrating the end of tourist season. Funny thing is, it's gotten so big that it brings all kinds of tourists back around. Anyway, you should stop back by if you're passing through and check it out."

"Sounds like fun. I'll have to see how long I need to stay home, but if I'm passing through, I will definitely stop by."

"Is everything okay back home?"

"Oh, yeah," I decided to answer with a different answer than what I'd been giving everyone else. "I just haven't been home in a while, and my sister just found out she's pregnant with her first kid, so of course she's freaking out."

I sat waiting for a response, or even a thought, and when neither came, I asked, "So, is it your job as town keeper to ask all the random passersby to stay for... um, what was it? The Post-Winter Festival?"

His broad shoulders shuddered with silent laughter. "Like I told you last night, I don't own the town."

"Why does Staci seem to think you do?"

"My family has been here a long time, and I happen to still own a couple of the original buildings."

"Only a couple of buildings," I repeated, mocking him flirtatiously. "What's the rest of your family doing in town if you own the buildings?"

"They're all gone now," he answered evenly. "I was an only child, so once my family passed away, I was all that was left."

I felt sorry for prying, which he noticed and quickly added, "Don't feel bad. They've all been gone a long time now, and that's life. The townspeople are my family now."

The waitress placed my eggs in front of me with good timing after I'd just put my foot in my mouth. While I ate, he told me more about the history of Logan and where his family came into the picture.

When I was done eating, I reached for my wallet, but Ben waved me off as he told the girl to put it on his tab.

"I can't let you do that, Ben."

"Of course you can... I know the owner," he said with a wink.

"Thank you," I responded. "I hate to eat and run, but I really should be getting on the road. It was nice talking to you and who knows, maybe I'll see you this weekend."

"I hope so," he said slowly. "I think you'll find it... enlightening."

NINE

I lay in my childhood bed, wide awake, the following Friday morning. Being home for four days had gotten me nowhere closer to figuring out why and how I was hearing people's thoughts. If anything, it made me dislike my problem even more. Hearing a stranger's thoughts while sitting next to them on the subway was one thing, but hearing my parents' thoughts was a whole different concept that I did not consider before coming home.

My parents were beyond thrilled when I arrived late Monday evening, but as the evening wore on, I quickly found myself regretting my decision to come home. I loved both my parents and had what I felt like were normal parents and a normal childhood growing up. They were supportive and made sure we were provided for properly. Our parents never held us back from following our dreams no matter what we decided to do.

Grace, my mother, was a small woman who had always maintained a short hairstyle, which over the years had turned from a light strawberry blonde to gray. She was always involved—and still is to this day—in anything and everything to do with our community. I considered her to be somewhat of a celebrity when I was growing up. She threw my sister, brother, and me into every sport, group, or fundraiser we could possibly imagine to keep us involved as well.

Bob, my father, was much taller than my mom and was recognizable in public by his unageing, thick, jet-black hair. He has held his position as branch manager at our local bank for over thirty years. Between the two of them in our small community, they were a powerhouse and loved by everyone.

I never knew them to be anything more than the loving, caring parents they'd always been—until Monday night at dinner. My mom's thoughts consisted of comments such as, *Why is she so thin? When will she come back home and settle down? This New York phase can't go on forever. Why can't she be more like Heidi!? What did I do wrong as a mother?*

My father's thoughts were along the same lines, as if they were sharing their thoughts with one another, and ended with him thinking, *I wonder if Riley would notice me grabbing her mom's butt... eh, who cares? I'm going to do it anyway.*

At that, I excused myself from the table and locked myself in the room for the rest of the night, using the excuse that I was tired from the long drive.

Now as I laid here, looking around at my adolescent boy-band posters and various awards from the different sports I'd participated in, I was reminded of a simpler time. I wondered how much longer I could stand staying here without making any progress.

I decided not to say anything to my parents about my predicament. For one thing, I didn't want to freak them out, and I also didn't want to draw any attention away from my sister's pregnancy. When they weren't internally bashing me for living so far away in a *dead-end career*, the new grandbaby was all they could think about.

I was so bold as to ask them if we knew of any witches in our family history—chalking it up to a book I'd read recently—which only resulted in odd stares and concerns that I may have gotten mixed in with the wrong crowd back in

New York. I let it go, knowing beforehand it was far-fetched, but I had to start somewhere.

I could hear my mom moving in the kitchen downstairs, but I wasn't ready to get up. I'd made the decision to head back to Logan today after talking it over with Ashley on the phone last night, but I hadn't told my parents yet. There was just something about Ben and the fact that I couldn't hear any of his thoughts. I felt it deep down in my bones that I needed to go back to find out what, if anything, that something was for myself.

Ashley agreed and said she didn't mind getting a flight back to New York. Then she added once that was cleared up, "So, are you going to grab a drink with Mark when you get back in town?"

I'd made the mistake of also mentioning my phone conversation with Mark the other night when I was in Logan.

"I don't know, Ashley. Doesn't that seem crazy?"

"Maybe a little, but you know me, I'm always up for crazy," she said. "What's the worst thing that could happen? You get a drink, realize you don't like hearing his thoughts, then you don't see him again."

"You're not wrong, but it still doesn't feel right," I responded.

"Well as much as I hate Nate, Mark was always nice."

"Good to know," I acknowledged.

"Tell me more about Ben."

I knew Ashley had been dying to know more about the handsome guy in the mysterious town. To avoid giving into my own musings over Ben since meeting him four days ago, I responded shortly, saying, "I've already told you all I know."

She had decided not to pry any further and that was the end of our phone call.

Today, my mom and I were going to have lunch at Vinny's, an Italian restaurant that we used to eat at often when I was younger. Over coffee, I broke the news to both my parents that I would be heading back to pick up Ashley after lunch. Once again, I hated lying—even though it was becoming easier to do—but it was better than telling them that I was going back to a small town in Oklahoma to meet up with a stranger I barely knew, and oh yes, I can hear people's thoughts now. No big deal, right?

I tried not to think about it as we walked into Vinny's, the smell of marinara sauce and toasted garlic bread heavy in the air. It was a seat yourself kind of restaurant, so as I was looking around for an open table, I heard my mom's thought mirror mine behind me as I saw my sister sitting at a table looking down at a menu. *Is that Heidi?*

At the same time, she looked up and saw us there, smiled, and waved us over.

"Heidi! What are you doing here?" I asked surprised but happy at the same time.

"Yes what a surprise!" Mom said as she sat down next to her. *How wonderful! I get to have lunch with both of my girls!*

"Well, you said Riley was leaving, and Dad told me you were coming here for lunch, so surprise!"

"I'm glad you could make it," I said.

Oh yeah, then where was my invite?

Being the youngest of us three, she always felt left out, even though she was the golden child. Heidi was seven years younger than me, and our brother was right in the middle. While my brother and I were the black sheep of the family, venturing out and leaving home as soon as we could, she was the one who stayed, settled down, and was now providing our mother with her first grandchild.

I still admired her though, sitting there, long brown hair curled over her shoulders, a plain but pretty smile on her face, and the glow of her pregnancy emanating from her like heat coming off a radiator.

"How did you get away from work?" my mom asked.

"Oh, being pregnant has its benefits. I told them I was feeling nauseous, so they let me leave early," she laughed.

"Heidi! That's not right!" Mom said disapprovingly, but despite herself added, "But I'm also glad you could make it. I haven't had both my girls in one place in a long time."

Before our food came, I caught them up on some of the projects I was working on at work, both of them smiling and nodding, but neither actually interested. The conversation eventually turned to all baby talk; baby names, decor for the nursery, what she needed to buy and do before the big day, things her doctor had told her, et cetera.

Just like they had felt about my work talk, I found the baby talk uninteresting. I was excited for my sister and her husband, Robert, but having a baby was something I couldn't even imagine right now, especially when I couldn't bring myself to date anyone. I still felt content listening to her plans for the future with her new little family. Even though I wasn't any closer to finding the answers I came home hoping to find, I was glad for the brief time with my family over the last few days.

As we pulled back into the driveway later, I saw my dad shutting the hood to my Jeep, a red rag with black oil stains on it dangling from the pocket of his jeans.

Damn kids not taking care of their damn cars, I heard him mutter as we greeted him.

"Riley, you need to take better care of your car, especially before going on a long road trip like this," he began. "I rotated the tires and changed the oil, so you should be good to go."

"Thanks, Dad," I said. "I'll try to be better about taking care of Betty."

Betty? Seriously Riley? He rolled his eyes and said, "Good."

"I'm going to go grab my bag so I can get on the road."

When I came back out, we said our goodbyes. I got in my car and pulled out of the driveway. I glanced back at them in my rearview mirror where they both stood, my mom waving to me, and I got the strangest feeling that I would never see them again.

I quickly pushed that feeling aside, knowing it was silly. I wasn't dying—that I knew of—I was only hearing people's thoughts without the slightest clue as to why. I circled back to the theory of having eaten or drank something on New Year's Eve to have caused this. However, since I was the only one affected by said powerful substance, I knew that couldn't be the cause of this.

I was so lost in thought on all the possible theories running through my mind that it took me half of the drive to realize that my dad had also cleaned the inside of my car for me. He wasn't wrong that I needed to take better care of Betty. She had been my first big-girl purchase after graduating from Yale. I used to dream of owning a beige, soft-topped Jeep, but when it came time to purchase one, I couldn't find one. The last lot that I looked in, I found Betty. The Jeep had a shiny jet-black exterior—hence the name Black Betty—and a beige interior, but no soft-top.

I ended up purchasing the black one anyway, proud of my new vehicle that I bought all by myself. In the beginning, I would clean her once a month and go for long drives on the weekends out of the city. She surprisingly didn't have many miles on her now for how old she was, but then again, after a few years living in the city, all she did now was sit parked on a side street, wrapped in a fabric car cover.

As I made my way closer to Logan, I started to second guess my decision to go back, but something inside of me was telling me to go. I didn't know what I was expecting to find out by going back, nor why I felt both nervous and eager to see Ben again. I tried to think of how our conversation would go.

He'd think I was nuts if I told him my secret and that I thought he had the answers to the questions I had been asking for two weeks now.

The sun had just gone down as I pulled once again into the driveway of the Black Horse Inn. This time the parking lot was full of vehicles, making me regret not calling to book a room ahead of time. Ben had warned me that the festival brought people from all over.

I took my chances and walked up the steps and through the French doors in the foyer, warm from the fire roaring in the fireplace. Trudy was behind the front desk looking down at the guestbook while carrying on a conversation with someone from the kitchen who was dressed like a chef.

She looked up as I approached, smiled, and said, "Hello, how can I help you?"

Why does she look so familiar? I heard before I could respond.

"Hi. I am hoping you still have a room available," I said, adding quickly, "I am here for the festival."

"Let me see… what is your name, sweetie?"

"Riley Bandoni."

"Oh, of course, Riley!" she said relieved. "I have your reservation right here. For tonight and tomorrow night, correct?"

Before I could question my reservation, her thoughts solved the mystery for me. *Mr. Blackwood will be so happy to know she made it back here!*

"Right…" was all I could say.

As I followed her to my room, I wondered if his confidence that I would return was a good sign that he knew something or if he wanted me to come back for strictly carnal reasons.

TEN

I settled into my new room—a different one than the one I had stayed in last weekend, with this room's theme being yellow—and glanced at the inn's restaurant menu lying on the bedside table. The menu looked appetizing, and I wanted to stall seeing Ben a little longer.

The inn was much livelier this week, with families and couples occupying every inch of the downstairs' shared areas. In the dining area I even noticed a few other people, like me, who seemed to be here alone.

Since the seating was limited, I ended up eating with a younger couple from Little Rock named John and Carol. They were here celebrating their fourth anniversary. They told me this was their first time coming to Logan, but they had friends who had visited before and loved it.

After dinner we all walked together along the path to town, which like the inn, was packed with people coming and going.

I began obsessing over what I was going to say to Ben when I saw him, so much that I barely remembered crossing the street to the town square. It wasn't until I almost ran into a crossing guard who was directing traffic that I saw the entire square packed with small rides and carnival booths, some of which were overflowing into the streets around the square. I navigated the sea of people toward Blacky's, where I was able to snag one empty chair at the end of the bar.

Tonight, there were two guys working behind the bar. One was a tall, burly guy with long uncombed hair and a beard. The other guy was much shorter with a clean, military buzz cut and shaven face. The burly one came over to take my order when I sat down.

"What can I get for you?" he said in a deep voice.

"Michelob, please."

Without saying anything, he walked away to grab my beer from the deep cooler behind the bar.

"Riley! You're back!" I heard a familiar voice behind me.

"Hey, Staci!" I said, turning around. "Yeah, I was heading home and decided I couldn't miss this amazing festival, so here I am."

Right... came back for the festival did you... she thought with a matching doubtful look on her face. "Right on," she said. "How were your folks?"

"They were good, happy to see me."

"That's good!" she said.

Someone in the back shouted her name, then she said, "I've got to run, busy night, but let me know if you need anything!"

"Sure thing!"

I sat there, sipping my beer and waiting for Ben's appearance. Every time the door to the back opened or someone walked in the front door, my heart sank a little. After two beers and no sign of Ben, I began to feel silly for coming at all.

I considered asking Staci where he was, but I didn't want to confirm her already suspicious thoughts that I came back just to see Ben, even if it was true. Instead, I decided to ask the big bartender next time he came to check on me. After all, he wouldn't know that I was here a few days ago.

"Hey, is Ben around?"

"No," he said shortly. *Is that what she's been waiting on all night?*

"Okay, thanks." I felt my cheeks turning red.

Staci snuck up behind me at the same time and said, "He's gone for the night picking up some stuff for tomorrow. He'll be back in the morning."

"Oh, alright." Eager to change the subject, I said, "Are there any live bands playing tonight or tomorrow?"

Poor thing doesn't realize she's got no chance with ol' Benjamin Blackwood. "Oh yes! It's actually a local band called..." she described the local band which consisted of a lawyer, accountant, the feed store owner, and an insurance agent. They all grew up together in town and formed the band as a joke a long time ago, though they became so good at performing covers, they kept the band going all these years.

"When I describe them, it sounds like a bad dad joke, but they're actually pretty good."

"Sounds like an interesting group," I laughed.

"They are that for sure," she answered. "Do you need another beer?"

"No, I think I'm going to get going, but I'll see you tomorrow."

"Yes, I'll be here!"

Later, lying in my fluffy, cream-colored bed, I wondered what Staci meant by me not having a chance with Ben... not that I was looking to *have a chance* with him, but it still made me wonder what she knew about him that I didn't know yet. He obviously wanted me to come back for a reason—he went out of his way to book me a room at the inn. However, he wasn't here on the day he assumed I would arrive.

I fell asleep quickly and dreamt yet again of a black horse running through a lush field.

The next day, I took my time exploring the trails that ran between the inn and town in the morning and made my way through the shops bordering the square in the evening. I snacked on greasy carnival food, not remembering the last time I'd had a funnel cake. More people flooded through the town as the sun set behind the buildings, the lights from the rides still illuminating a day-like glow over the town.

I sat at a bench on the outskirts of the commotion, observing the mass chaos of people coming and going. I was beginning to wonder if I'd ever get a chance to talk to Ben or if coming back here was a mistake when I heard his voice behind me say, "You made it!"

"I did," I said after turning around. I found myself looking up at him, standing with his hands in his jacket pockets, smiling down at me, just as handsome as the last time I'd seen him. His dark auburn hair was now a bright red in the carnival lights.

"You weren't kidding. The festival is pretty cool," I offered as he sat down next to me.

"Yeah, it has become a pretty big hit over the years," he said, staring out into the crowds in front of us.

"Thank you for reserving a room for me at the inn," I said. "You didn't have to do that."

"No problem at all. I was hoping you'd come back, and I know how quickly it books up."

I blushed, hoping he didn't notice.

"Are you having a good time?" he asked.

"Yes, everyone is so nice here." I hesitated before adding, "I've missed that... being in a small town where everyone treats you like family. Plus, it's been nice to just slow down."

"I get that. I lived in New York once. Wonderful place but you'll definitely get left behind if you don't keep up with the flow."

"For sure. I remember my whole first year living there was a mix of every emotion between fear and excitement," I said, laughing a little to myself, causing his smile to return as well.

"Sounds about right for New York."

"Why did you leave New York?" I asked after a moment.

The smile faded slightly from his face as he responded, "Times were getting tough in the city, and I was ready to slow down."

"I know what you mean."

Screams from kids on the bigger rides followed by laughter distracted us for a moment.

Ben broke the silence a minute later. "Do you want to grab a drink?"

"Sure."

I assumed he was leading me toward Blacky's, but we kept walking, and he led us around the corner to the next street over. There were more shops and restaurants on this street, but with fewer people. The noise from the carnival died away significantly as we walked further along the street toward a small hole-in-the-wall bar suitably named The Hideaway.

Ben held the door open for me as I entered the small pub, whose interior decor closely resembled that of Blacky's but on a much smaller scale. I also noticed there was no kitchen here, only five tables and a short bar.

"We opened this place for the locals to go to when the town is packed with tourists," he said.

I wasn't sure if he was offering information on his choice of location or if he noticed me looking around, observing its similarities to Blacky's. I considered the idea of him being able to hear *my* thoughts and that being the reason he wanted me to come back to Logan. I knew that seemed a it of a stretch since I couldn't hear his thoughts, but I had a feeling that I'd find out soon enough.

Only one of the five tables at The Hideaway was occupied by two men and two women who briefly greeted Ben when he entered. The men were listening to a baseball game on a small radio while their wives chatted about what sounded like the latest town gossip. They paused their banter as Ben and I walked past them, staring curiously at me.

Who is that young lady with Ben?

Is that sweet boy finally seeing someone? He deserves it.

Luckily where we sat at the bar was far enough away that I couldn't hear any more thoughts from the two women.

There was an older gentleman sitting behind the bar reading a newspaper from another town. His hair was grayed out and braided into a long ponytail down his back. He was wearing faded blue jeans and a colorful Hawaiian button-down. He barely glanced over his reading glasses as Ben walked behind the bar and greeted him. "How's it going, Daryl?"

He grunted something close to the word fine before returning his gaze to the newspaper.

"What would you like?" Ben asked me as he reached down into a cooler.

"Any beer is fine," I said, and he placed two bottles on the counter for both of us.

Daryl handed him a bottle opener from his pocket without being asked or looking up from his paper.

"Staci seems like a great person," I offered when Ben sat down.

"Yeah," he said, taking a sip of his beer. "She is. I don't know what I'd do without her."

"Are you and her—" I started, knowing very well what the answer was but hoping to get some more information out of him.

"Dating?" he said surprised. "No. She's like a younger sister to me. I helped her out when she had nowhere else to go, and now I can't get rid of her."

I laughed, knowing he was joking, but he added anyway, "I'm only kidding. She really is a great person and has made an impression on the people in town here. Sweet as can be and always willing to help anyone."

"I can tell," I said, taking a sip of my beer.

"What's your story, Riley?" he asked after a moment.

"What do you mean?" I hesitated, my heart sinking a little into my stomach. He didn't answer, so I said, "I have no crazy story. I'm from a small town in Texas and moved to New York after college for work."

"What do you do?"

"I manage my own marketing team at one of the big marketing firms in the city," I said.

"That sounds interesting," Ben said smiling like he'd just won a prize.

I explained some of the projects that my team and I had worked on in the last year or two, and he sat listening intently. I forgot how nice it was to have a conversation with someone whose thoughts I couldn't hear while I was talking.

I stopped when I realized that I'd been droning on about my job for over ten minutes. "I'm sorry. I don't mean to bore you with the details of my job."

"No, don't be. I've learned something new about the marketing industry."

"You don't have to be so nice about it," I said laughing. "Didn't you say you lived in New York at one point?"

"I did."

"What brought you to the big city?"

"Work," he said simply. "I was helping with a big construction project going on in the city for a couple of years. After that there was nothing there for me, so I left and came back down here."

We had two more beers, during which time we talked about where we grew up, life in New York, and how it was living in Logan. He was charming and sweet but very reserved. When he spoke about his childhood and the town, he seemed vague about certain details. I didn't question it but listened as I found him wildly intriguing at the same time.

After our third beer and a pause in the conversation, I was bold enough to say, "I have to ask . . ."

"Yes?" he said facing me, interlacing his fingers, one elbow on the counter and one on the back of the barstool, his broad shoulders puffing out of his shirt.

"Do you treat all your tourists with this unique hospitality?"

His mouth curved up into a half a smile, and he took his last sip of his beer. "No, I don't. I just found myself wanting to know more about you."

Between the beer and the alluring way he spoke, my face felt red-hot. "Why?"

Without saying a word, he stood up and offered me his hand. "Let's go for a walk."

"What?"

"Come on, trust me."

My common sense was screaming not to go anywhere with a stranger, but his friendly smile and captivating green eyes shunned my better judgement.

I took his hand and followed him out of the bar.

Eleven

We walked in silence toward the trail leading back to the Black Horse Inn, the noises from the fair fading away as we edged further away from town. There were still groups of people walking along the trail, so we weren't completely isolated from others.

Before we crossed the bridge that went over the creek, Ben slowed down and turned down a trail leading off the main path.

I hesitated, my inner voices still arguing with one another; one telling me to run and the other telling me to keep following him.

"Don't worry, I'm not going to hurt you," he said softly, noticing my hesitation.

"Isn't that what a serial killer might say right before they murder you?"

He laughed, which made me relax a little. Once again, I found myself desperately wishing that I could hear his thoughts but at the same time, I felt an overwhelming sense of trust toward him. He continued walking, and I followed behind—just in case he was a nutjob.

I could hear the creek bubbling to the left of us, following along the same trail that we were walking down. Within minutes, the path opened to what looked like a small park at the edge of a large lake. The night was clear enough that the moon was providing most of the lighting on the lake and the park. There were a few dimly lit light poles illuminating above several picnic tables scattered around the area. I could also barely make out groups of benches placed around firepits in between the picnic tables.

It was quiet, except for the distant cries of children on the carnival rides and crickets chirping. I was slightly surprised to see that no one else was out here enjoying the placid lake view.

"At least you bring your victims to a peaceful spot," I joked, trying to ease my own tension.

He laughed out loud this time but said nothing until we sat down at a picnic table facing the water.

"I've lived here for a long time, and this has always been my favorite place to come and read or think or sometimes just sit in silence. It's the one place that hasn't changed, ever."

"You speak as if you've been here for hundreds of years."

There was a long pause before he said, "Would you believe me if I told you I have?"

The smile on his face was gone, making it difficult to gauge if he was serious or not. I answered anyway. "No." When he didn't say anything, I asked, "Why did you want to bring me out here?"

"To show you this." He gestured toward the lake.

"Well, yes, it's beautiful, but I don't believe you."

"Why are you here, Riley?" he asked pointedly.

"What do you mean? You brought me here."

"No, I mean here, in Logan." He turned to face me now.

"I told you; I was on my way home to visit my parents when I found Logan while looking for gas and a place to sleep," I said, confused. "Why?"

"You'd never heard of Logan or me before coming here?"

My heart started racing, beating erratically in my ears. "Am I missing something?" I said.

"If you are who I think you are, something happened to you recently. A big change in your life that you can't explain."

Then my heart stopped altogether for a second, and resumed pounding heavily in my ears as I hopped off the bench, staring wild-eyed at him. I didn't know what to say; a part of me thought for a second that he could be referring to something—or someone else—and if I admitted my secret, then I was exposing myself to a complete stranger. Another part of me considered the possibility that I stumbled upon someone like me by random chance. I felt hot despite the cool weather, and I was shaking slightly. I began pacing back and forth while Ben sat there motionless.

Before I could come up with a proper response, he said, "You're not alone, Riley."

I stopped pacing and stood there, speechless.

"Here, sit back down and I'll explain," he said calmly.

I didn't want to sit. I wanted answers. I said the first thing that came to my mind, "What do you mean I'm not alone?"

"There are others like you... Ten of us to be exact."

At this, I sat back down on the picnic table, my mind racing and trying to register what he was saying.

He asked in a tone that insinuated this wasn't news for him, "Tell me what you've figured out so far."

"Well, I uhm... I'm not... I don't—" I knew I was babbling, so I took a deep breath to compose myself. "Apparently not much, considering I didn't even know there were others. I mean the thought crossed my mind, but I wasn't sure," I continued more calmly. "Two weeks ago on New Year's Eve, it was as if a switch flipped, and next thing I know, I'm hearing people's thoughts."

He waited.

"You said what have I figured out? Is there more to this than me hearing people's thoughts? Can you hear people's thoughts too?"

"No," he said plainly. "We all have a different ability. Mine is strength."

"Strength?" I repeated. "Like Superman?"

"Yes and no. I have my limits, but... well, it would be easier to show you."

He stood up and looked around, I assumed to make sure no one was near, and walked over to another picnic table sitting a few feet from ours. He lifted the entire table over his head with one hand as if he were lifting a duffle bag full of clothes. I could see the muscles in his arms barely straining to hold the table, and his face remained soft, staring at me. He finally placed the picnic table back on the ground and walked back toward me.

I knew my mouth was hanging open. Still in disbelief, I stood up and walked over to the table to make sure he wasn't playing a joke on me. Sure enough, the table was solid wood, and I struggled to lift it more than a hair off the ground.

I could hear him snickering behind me.

"How is this possible? Why are we like this? How does it happen? Does this mean I'm some kind of superhero now or something?"

I was blurting out the questions as they were forming in my head until he interrupted me by holding up his hands to stop me.

"Hold on, one question at a time. But first, you should know that I don't have all the answers. What I can tell you is that our abilities transfer to another person when we die, which usually isn't that often. We don't really know the how or the why, but as far as we've figured out, this has been happening for at least a thousand years... maybe longer," he said. Then he continued, "We're not superheroes. For the most part, we keep ourselves hidden. None of us wants to become someone else's science project, if you know what I mean."

I nodded and waited for him to tell me more. When nothing came, I said, "This doesn't make any sense."

"I know. It took me a while to get used to it as well."

"So you didn't *change* a few weeks ago when I did?"

"Um, no." Ben scanned my face, probably trying to figure out how much more I could handle. Then he said, "There's one more thing. When we get our ability, we stop aging."

This time I thought for sure he was joking with me. When he didn't laugh, I asked, "What do you mean we stop aging?"

"I got my ability on my thirty-seventh birthday... two hundred and five years ago... I was born in 1757."

He was quiet as I processed this unexpected new piece of information. I felt in denial rather than shocked. "You're joking with me, right?" I started. "Obviously you have superhuman strength, but you mean to tell me that you're two hundred years old?! That's impossible!"

I thought briefly to myself, so is hearing people's thoughts and having superhuman strength.

"I wish I could say that I was," Ben said calmly. "I didn't believe it at first either, but it's true. Luckily, you get to hear it from me now before it takes you years to figure it out on your own."

"What do you mean?"

"Well, I didn't have someone to tell me what was happening to me. At first, having extra strength was strange, but I got used to it after a while and it became normal—to me at least." He paused before continuing, "It wasn't until I began outliving others that I knew something was different about me. I never changed; I never grew older. Unfortunately, I didn't meet anyone else like me for another hundred years.

"In 1918, I met Odin—he's the oldest one of all of us—and he explained what I've just told you; about the others, their abilities, how we don't age, and what the visions meant. It all finally made sense, and I remember feeling relieved that I wasn't alone."

I had completely forgotten about the dream from the other night. "The dream... from the other night... you had it too?"

"We all have the same vision—or dream—whatever you want to call it. When one of us dies, the ability transfers to someone new at midnight on their birthday following the other one's death. The dream tells us who has passed and to whom their ability is transferring to. Then we track down the new ones when they change and let them know what they are now. Like what we're doing now."

"But no one has come to me..."

"Give us a break! It's only been two weeks," he laughed. "All we have is a first and last name to go off of, so sometimes it takes time to find someone."

I didn't respond, but he said exactly what I was thinking.

"What I can't figure out is how you found me first."

"Ben, none of this makes sense, so why should that make sense either!?"

"I guess you're right," he said with a smirk.

We both stared out toward the lake for a few minutes.

"Is this why I can't hear your thoughts?"

"Yes," he answered. "Peter once told me that he liked being around us the most because he couldn't hear any of our thoughts, and it was the one time he felt normal."

"Who's Peter?" I said before I could catch myself from asking a dumb question.

"The one you received your ability from."

"Right... Did you know who I was last week at Blacky's when we met?"

"Sort of," he began. "I recognized your name from the dream obviously, so after I'd left, I called Elliot. He's another one of us who does most of the tracking. He works for the

FBI and has access to their databases to find people. Anyway, I asked him if he'd found Riley Bandoni yet, to which he said he'd narrowed it down to one in Montana and another in New York. I figured it was too much of a coincidence that a Riley Bandoni from New York was in my bar so soon after a change, so I took a chance."

"Why didn't you tell me all of this last week? You would have saved me a lot of disturbing thoughts from my parents over the last week."

He grinned and said, "By the time I figured out it was you, you were already gone. I hoped you'd come back this weekend, otherwise one of us would've met up with you in New York anyway. But here we are."

"Here we are indeed." I wasn't sure what else to ask at this point. Instead, I listened to the crickets and the frogs battling it out on who was the loudest lake creature. "You said Odin is the oldest. How old is he?"

"Let's see..." he said coolly, "I think he's just over a thousand years old now."

"One thousand years old! That's impossible! You mean to tell me this guy has just been roaming the Earth for over a thousand years unnoticed?"

"Yes."

"I'm supposed to believe that it's possible for me to also live a thousand years as well?"

"You may if you can avoid dying," he said casually.

"Wait, so we can still die? Well, obviously because then the abilities wouldn't transfer."

"We're not immortal. We just stop aging." He stopped before adding, "We're still susceptible to any kind of death except being able to die of old age."

"None of this make sense. It goes against human nature!"

"Trust me, I thought the same thing. But here I am two hundred years later."

"Are the others here in town?" I asked.

"No, only me," he said. "However, they all consider Logan to be a sort of safe haven when they need to get away or when we just need to check in on one another occasionally. Like I said before, we don't get new people very often. We're fairly good at laying low and staying alive."

Just then another thought occurred to me. "You say the ability transfers when one *passes* . . . but you also keep saying that you don't usually get new ones often because everyone is good at staying alive..."

I didn't need the ability to read minds to know that the look on his face matched my train of thought.

"You catch on quick, Riley," he said. "That's two new people in less than two weeks. *That* I have no explanation for, but it's on all our minds. It's never happened as far as I know of, and maybe it's just coincidence or maybe..."

He trailed off, trying to decide if he wanted to share his theory with me or not. Ultimately, he must have decided not to because he stood up and offered his hand to me once again. "It's most likely nothing. It's getting late. I'll walk you back to the inn."

I still had more questions, but even without looking at my watch I knew it was well past midnight, and I wasn't sure how much more information I could handle tonight. I took his hand and stood. Before we could make our way back to the trail, I stopped and said, "I have one more question."

He looked down at me intently, his handsome face searching mine in the moonlight.

"What do I do now?" I asked simply.

He waited a moment before responding, "Whatever you want. Some of us believe these abilities are gifts to lead an extraordinary life, and some of us live without questioning the why behind it all."

"Which one of those do you believe?"

"I believe that everything happens for a reason and that you don't need a supernatural ability or to stop aging to live an exceptional life. Although, I can't say that I've complained much about having either of those things either." He winked and added, "But that's just me."

Before I knew it, we were walking through the courtyard behind the inn. It was quiet and most of the lights inside were off. I had glanced at my watch on the walk back from the lake and saw that it was one o'clock in the morning.

Ben stayed at the bottom of the steps as I made my way up to the back door.

I turned around at the top to tell him goodnight when he said first, "Do you want to grab breakfast in the morning?"

"I'd like that," I said, smiling. "Thank you for tonight."

He smiled and said, "Goodnight, Riley."

Then he disappeared into the dark cascade of the night, heading back in the direction toward town.

Twelve

Despite how late it was and how mentally exhausted I felt, I couldn't sleep. The idea of hearing people's thoughts was one thing, but now knowing I had the potential to live for a very long time was almost too much to comprehend. This was also considering the fact that I had to avoid being killed to stay thirty forever.

Most women would kill to remain thirty forever, I thought to myself.

Another thing bothering me was the odd coincidence of ending up in Logan and finding Ben. I thought back to the road construction in Dallas, causing me to detour through Oklahoma City and how my gas ran low at exactly the right time as I approached the exit for Logan.

All of this was surreal and strange.

Knowing that this was my new normal, I tried to decide if I would tell Ashley what I had found out. She already knew about me hearing thoughts, but I debated on telling her about the others and living forever. I knew I could trust her, but by telling her I would be exposing the others' secret as well.

My last thought before finally dozing off was how good Ben looked for a two hundred and something year old.

***

I was abruptly woken up at eight in the morning by the piercing sound of the bedside alarm. For a split second, I thought last night might have been a dream, but I knew better than that.

I grabbed a to-go cup of coffee from the inn's dining room and headed into town, anxious to see Ben again. I'd come up with more questions that I wanted to ask him before I headed back to New York—something I'd decided on last night before falling asleep.

All the carnival rides and booths were very still in the morning fog that lay around them, giving the town a sinister look.

I spotted Ben and Staci sitting on a bench outside of Blacky's discussing work. Staci was holding a stack of papers in her lap.

"Good morning," I said as I approached them.

Ben looked up and showed his dazzling smile, while Staci looked surprised to see me and said, "Well, hello there!" *Dang, she looks like she had a rough night.*

"Hi. I was just about to head over there to see if you were up yet," Ben said. "Give us a minute to finish up here, and then we can grab breakfast."

Staci gave him a sideways look, suspicious of our early morning meeting plans. *Breakfast? Maybe that's why she looks rough... didn't get much sleep thanks to ol' Benji, huh?*

"No problem, take your time." I turned away before Staci could see me blush and walked far enough away to be out of range of her thoughts, sipping my coffee.

"Order more ground meat from that beef guy near Oklahoma City. I'll go pick it up next week. No more turkey burgers. No one wants that crap," I could barely hear Ben telling Staci as she wrote down his instructions.

"Got it boss!" she said and got up to leave. "You two kids enjoy breakfast."

"You ready?" Ben said.

"Yes, I'm starving."

When Staci was out of earshot, Ben murmured, "She thinks we hooked up last night, doesn't she?"

He looked as if this was the funniest thing in the world, while I could feel my face turning red again.

"Yes," I said smirking.

"Don't worry about it," he said.

"Well, I don't want everyone to think I'm some kind of harlot that rolled into town just to bag the unattainable Ben Blackwood."

"Unattainable?"

I smiled, and ignored his comment. Instead I asked, "So, where are we having breakfast?"

"Cal's. It's over there on the corner."

He led the way. Once inside, we sat down at a table by the window, away from the few other people enjoying their breakfast.

The waitress, a young girl with short, curly brown hair wearing a red plaid apron brought us over two cups of coffee and a basket of biscuits. Betty—read the name tag pinned to her shirt—had a crush on Ben but he didn't seem to notice.

Once she was gone, I began, "Why doesn't Staci know about you?"

"I've learned over time that there isn't any point in telling people," he said without elaborating why.

"How do people not notice you... you know, not growing older?"

"Every couple of decades, I go away for a while and then come back as a long-lost son or something. Not many people question it, and it's worked so far." He took a sip of coffee and glanced out of the window.

"You really do own the town."

It wasn't a question, but he answered quietly, "I started the town in 1896. It was after I left New York. I was ready to find a place to settle with a few other people who left New York with me. I acquired roughly three thousand acres, and we've been here ever since. I've helped out where I can, and the people are the ones who have made the town what it is today. When new people come along, people tell them my father, grandfather, or great-grandfather owned such and such building, them not knowing it has always just been me."

"That's crazy that you've been able to get away with that for so long here."

He didn't say anything but smiled.

"I think I'm going to go back to New York."

"Understandable," he said.

Our food came and we ate in silence while watching workers trickle into the town square to break down the carnival rides and booths.

I felt his eyes on me, waiting for me to ask more questions, but all the questions I'd thought of this morning were gone. I didn't know what else I could ask that may make this feel normal.

"I know how you're feeling." He placed his hand over mine, which was sitting on the table. "You're relieved and confused at the same time. I promise it will get easier even if life doesn't seem like it will ever feel normal again."

His hand was warm on mine, and I smiled, heart pounding from his touch. "Easier said than done."

After we were done, Betty passed back by to grab our empty plates, and Ben asked her for a pen and paper, which she eagerly handed him from her pocket.

He wrote down the number to Blacky's and said, "If you need to talk or come up with more questions, please don't hesitate to call."

"Thank you," I said, taking the paper from him.

"Also, the others will want to meet you eventually when you're ready. It may help meeting the others, not just me."

"I'll keep that in mind. Right now, I just need to—"

"I know. Take your time."

"Ben..." I started.

"Yes?"

"I know I said it last night but thank you again for telling me all of this. I went home trying to find answers and somehow—still not sure how—I found you. I'm still confused as hell, but you've made it a little easier to accept."

"Of course. We have to watch out for one another." He smiled big enough to show his perfect white teeth.

"I have to ask," I began, "is it bad if one person knows about me?"

Before he could answer, I explained, "My roommate kind of figured out the mind reading thing before I did the night that it happened."

"It's not *bad*. You can choose to tell whoever you want, whatever you want. I would just be careful who you choose to tell going forward. As I am sure you've already figured out, it's not just your secret anymore."

We parted ways in the street, and I was thankful for a lonely walk back to the inn. I could see how this town was everyone's safe haven. It was peaceful, and the people here were beyond nice and welcoming. I stopped at the bridge over the creek one last time, taking a deep breath. Once back in my room, I packed my bag and headed out of town back toward New York.

My goal was to make it as far as Columbus before stopping to rest, but as I approached Columbus later that evening, I blazed past every exit sign, determined to make it home. A part of me thought that once I made it back home, I'd begin to feel some sense of normalcy again. Another part of me thought I was an idiot to believe that first part.

I stopped at a rest stop somewhere in Pennsylvania around three in the morning and allowed myself to sleep for an hour before getting back on the road shortly before the sun began to rise in front of me.

I finally weaved my way through the streets of Manhattan mid-morning, and as I turned down our street, I was glad to see my parking spot was still open. I stumbled into the apartment too tired to think about anything else, and I made it as far as the couch before crashing face down on a white fluffy throw pillow purchased by Ashley last spring.

It felt as if I had only been sleeping for a few minutes when I was woken up by Ashley trying to let herself in the door to the apartment at five o'clock that evening. The apartment was darker from the now setting sun.

Damn, stupid, old rusted out lock! Open already!

I could hear her fussing to herself through the door that only ever gave her trouble. I still felt groggy, but I got up and unlocked the door for her.

What the— "Riley! You're back!" she shouted after seeing me open the door.

"I am," I said as she hugged me.

Before she was completely through the door, she started, "When did you get back? Did you find anything out? Did you ever go back to Logan? Also, what is up with you and Mark? He's called here twice to see if you're back yet."

"I will be happy to answer all of your questions after a shower, a beer, and some food."

Johnny's it is! she thought, grinning ear to ear.

"You read my mind."

We were at Johnny's less than an hour later, where Ashley filled me in on her week spent back at home. I made it through two beers and six chicken wings before she finished.

Wouldn't be time well spent back home without some family drama.

"I hear that," I said, realizing too late that I had responded to her thought.

"I have to say, as much as I missed you, I didn't miss... you know," she said pointing to her head.

"Yeah, I know what you mean. I am getting better at drowning it out, but it's not always perfect. I still hear things that I don't want to hear," I said, taking a sip of beer. "Five days with my parents was long enough."

She laughed. "I can't even imagine."

"Lucky you." I couldn't help but laugh with her. "How was work today?"

Of course you ask me about work first.

She rolled her eyes before finally saying, "Work was fine today. I had a lot to catch up on, but Tyler is running the team like a pro."

"Good to hear. That's why I left him in charge."

Get to the good stuff already!

"Ash, I don't know what you're talking about."

"You come home sooner than I expected you to, and I know you went back to Logan, so what did you find out?"

"Do you want another beer?" I said as I got up to order another round of drinks.

That good, huh?

"It's not like that," I said when I returned. "I didn't find anything out. I went back to Logan; the Ben guy wasn't there. I stayed for a day or two and decided to come home."

"That's it?" she said disappointed.

"That's it." I felt awful lying to her, but I had decided on the long drive back home to keep her in the dark about the rest. I figured that there was no reason she needed to know more than she already did.

"That sucks," she said. "What now?"

I'd been asking myself the same question and hadn't produced a good enough answer except to keep moving forward with the life I had before all of this happened.

I shrugged my shoulders in response to her question.

"I feel like you should be out fighting crime or something."

"The streets of New York do not need Riley Bandoni out there fighting crime by reading minds."

Ashley and I started laughing, both imagining me in a superhero costume.

"Have you been to the gym since you got back home?" I asked.

She knew what I was really asking and took a sip of her beer before answering. "Do you mean, have I seen Nate and kicked him in the nuts?"

I almost spit out the sip of beer that I'd just taken. "You kicked him in the nuts?"

"No, but I've played the scenario out in my mind a hundred times. Unfortunately, he's never alone at the gym long enough for me to do it. His band of followers never left his side when I went Saturday, and yesterday when I went, he and Natalie were making out the entire time on one of the machines."

"Oh Ash, I'm so sorry," I said. "Why don't you find a new gym or go at a different time and stop torturing yourself?"

"Seeing him has actually made my workouts more intense, so it's not total torture," she said as she grabbed another fry off the plate in front of her.

Once we were back home, Ashley handed me the messages that Mark had left during the week.

"Are you going to call him back?"

"I don't know," I answered honestly.

"When are you planning to come back to work?"

"Why? Does Fred miss me?"

"I wouldn't say that he misses you, but he does still seem pissed that you took time off without notice." *Not that I blame you.*

I wasn't looking forward to going back to work, but I had my answers, so there was no reason to delay trying to get back to normal.

"Tomorrow," I said finally.

"Tomorrow? Already?" she said surprised.

"Yes, there's no point in sitting around all day contemplating... things."

She stared blankly at me, no response or thoughts given.

"What?" I asked, sounding a little more irritated than I intended.

"You just seem content for someone who didn't find any answers."

"I've just had a lot of time to think over the last week, and I figured if I can't get answers, I need find a way to live with it," I said as I grabbed my bag off the ground next to the couch and started making my way toward my bedroom.

If you say so, I heard.

"I do," I said. "Well, I'm tired. I'll see you in the morning."

Thirteen

Work began to feel normal again after a couple of weeks—as normal as normal could be when you can hear everyone's thoughts.

I took advantage of my ability both with clients and my coworkers. In their eyes, I was doing all the right things by knowing what they were thinking without them knowing that I knew what they were thinking. At first, I felt guilty for intruding on their private thoughts, but I learned quickly when to ignore them and when to home in on the more important points.

I was only successful with my gift at work though. Going out in public was a bit trickier, and I found it difficult to be around strangers, especially when we were at the bar. The idea of dating anyone seemed more far-fetched the more I encountered people.

I'd ignored two more calls from Mark in the month since I'd been back home. I didn't think that he knew I was back. There was no way he'd know unless he followed me, but it had been over a week since his last attempt. I figured he'd finally given up.

"Are you ready for your Tuesday afternoon pick-me-up?" Ashley asked, snapping me out of my thoughts, as she stood in the doorway to my office.

"Yes!" I said. "I'll go today though. I need to get out of the office for a while."

Yeah, you seem distracted today.

"How so?"

"I stood here for almost two minutes before asking if you wanted coffee."

"Oh," I shot her a half smile. "I just have a lot on my mind. Same as usual for you?"

Yes.

I'd asked her to stop communicating through her thoughts with me at work, but I knew she couldn't always help it.

"I'll be back in a bit," I said as I grabbed my coat hanging by the door.

As I walked into the coffee shop, I noticed two things: one, the line was unusually long for this time of day, and two, Mark was sitting at a table near the window reading a *Forbes* magazine.

I considered turning around and walking out before he could see me, but it was too late. A big grin spread across his face as he picked me out from the crowd and waved at me. I waved back sheepishly and smiled. I had forgotten how attractive he was all those nights ago when we last saw one another.

He closed his magazine, threw his work bag over his shoulder, and walked toward me. Before he approached, I tried to think of a good excuse for not returning his phone calls and came up with zilch.

"Hey there, stranger," he said, the dimple on his cheek showing. *I wonder when she got back into town and if she was ever really gone.*

"Hi there!" I said a little too loudly. "How have you been?"

"I've been good, just busy with work as usual." *Lame. Ask her when she got back.* "How about you?" he added. "I take it you had a good trip home?" *Smooth.*

"Yes I did. It was nice to see my family, especially since I couldn't make it home over the holidays."

"That's good." He continued smiling. *So why have you been dodging my calls?*

"Look, I'm sorry that I haven't called you back. I've had a lot on my mind since I got back into town and work has been horribly busy." Neither of those excuses were technically lies.

Sounds like excuses to me.

"I know it sounds like a bunch of excuses," I said. He looked startled that I was responding to his thoughts but not bothered by it. "But I promise it's not. I had a great time New Year's Eve, and while I know this is the oldest excuse in the book, life is just a little too complicated right now for me to be seeing anyone."

"Maybe I like complicated," he said before criticizing himself. *Maybe I like complicated—what the hell, Mark?*

Luckily, it was my turn to order, delaying me from answering him and also allowing me to hide my smirk at him reprimanding himself.

"One medium black coffee and a medium cappuccino please."

"That'll be $8.26."

As I reached into my purse for my wallet, Mark stepped forward and handed his credit card to the barista. "Make that *two* black coffees and a cappuccino please."

"You didn't have to do that, ya know," I said, "but thank you."

"What kind of gentleman would I be if I let you buy my coffee?"

I chuckled and thought that he was full of it.

"Who's the black coffee for?"

"Me," I said as the barista handed us our coffees.

He held up the cappuccino and asked, "Then who's this one for?"

"My boyfriend," I teased as I headed toward door, leaving him standing there in shock.

Her boyfriend?! I heard before he chased me out the door and shouted, "Hold on! Wait a minute!"

By the time he caught up to me, he saw that I was laughing hysterically.

"Oh, someone's got jokes, do they?"

"The look on your face was well worth it," I said between laughs. "The cappuccino is for Ashley."

"Ashley..." he said, "the girl that introduced us who follows Nate around like a puppy?"

"I wouldn't say that she follows him around like a puppy, but yes, that's the same girl."

She followed him around like a puppy, and him being the jackass that he is, let her do it.

"Well, I need to get back to work," I said, reaching for the cappuccino he was still holding.

Instead, he held onto it and started walking in the direction of my office building. "Tell me more about your trip home."

I filled him in on visiting my parents and seeing my pregnant sister, obviously leaving out the bigger details of why I went home and visiting a small town called Logan, not once, but twice. He listened intently and without a thought. I stopped outside the entrance to my building and faced him.

"This is me," I said, pointing to the building behind me.

He finally handed me Ashley's cappuccino, and I added, "You're not going to stalk me now that you know where I work, are you?"

Mark said without thinking, "Only if you don't agree to let me take you out to dinner on Sunday."

"Dinner? On Sunday?"

"That's what I said."

I really wanted to say yes, but all my worries about dating someone whose thoughts I could hear were shouting at the forefront of my mind.

I heard, *That's not a no.* Then he said, "I'll pick you up at six on Sunday."

He left me standing outside the doors to my office building, feeling slightly elated and extremely apprehensive about our date on Sunday.

***

"Do you know what you're going to wear yet?" Ashley asked me during a commercial break of *Whose Line Is It Anyway?* the following night.

"No," I answered reluctantly, "I don't even know where he is taking me."

"Well, don't wear that sexy red dress you have—the one with the slit up the side—unless you want to be a cliche."

"A cliche?" I said, not understanding what she meant.

"Yeah," she responded with the same confused look on her face as me. *Because it's Valentine's Day...*

"What?!" I said loudly. "Oh crap!" How did I not realize that I'd agreed to go on a date with Mark on Valentine's Day!?

"You didn't realize it was Valentine's Day, did you?" she said giggling.

"No, of course not!" I was stunned. "I never would've agreed to go!"

"Going on a date on Valentine's Day isn't that bad, especially with him."

I rolled my eyes.

"Why are you so against dating him anyway?" she asked and then added the next fact as if it should've been a no brainer to date Mark. "He's dreamy and he's rich."

"You know why I'm against it," I said.

"I think it's great," she started. "Now you'll know what guys are thinking…"—*Who they're thinking about other than you*—"You can tell if you're wasting your time or not," she ended soberly.

I knew she wished that she had this kind of power over men and one man in particular. Even after what happened on New Year's Eve, she still wanted Nate back.

He called her last week—around midnight—begging her to come over to his place. His excuse for the New Year's Eve incident was that he thought it was her he was kissing, not Natalie. She didn't go over there due to my strong opinion of his excuse being a big load of crap. She hadn't heard from him since.

In her mind, by not going over there she had ruined any chance of a future relationship with him. I thought not answering his booty call was the best thing that could've happened.

"So no red?" I asked, changing the subject.

"No red," Ashley agreed and then added more excitedly, "Oo, wear that tight black dress, the one with the sparkles. I can loan you my six-inch heels."

"I like that dress, but no thanks on the heels. I don't want to break my neck."

✳✳✳

The night of my date with Mark was finally here. I was ready and had thirty minutes to spare before he arrived. I spent most of that time pacing and regretting my decision to go on this date. Ashley had left earlier to go to the gym, so I didn't have anyone to talk me down.

I'd done everything from folding clothes to putting away the dishes. I was in the process of picking up a book to read when the buzzer rang, announcing Mark's arrival.

I walked over to the window to make sure it was him before buzzing him up, not believing what I saw waiting down below. I ran to the call box and buzzed him up.

A few minutes later, Mark was knocking on the door.

I opened it slowly and said, "Hi."

"Hi," he said back. *Damn.*

I felt the heat rising in my cheeks. He, too, looked even more handsome than usual, dressed in slacks and a blazer.

"Are you ready?" he asked.

"Yes, let me just grab my jacket and purse."

Downstairs, I stood next to a limo the color of black velvet, waiting on the driver, who was wearing a black suit, to open the door for Mark and me.

"After you," said Mark.

I slid into the backseat, trying to contain my childish delight at being in a limo for the first time ever and failing miserably.

My eyes wandered over the mini bar, where crystal glasses sparkled in the overhead cab lighting and tiny bottles of every liquor imaginable were neatly lined up. When Mark slid in next to me, I was lost in thought, staring up at the sunroof, imagining myself re-enacting a scene from an old romance movie where the girl rode through Times Square hanging halfway out the sunroof as if she were flying.

I guess she hasn't ridden in a limo very much.

I caught him watching me and laughed at myself, slightly embarrassed.

Or ever.

He smiled at me, and I admitted, "Okay, so I've never been in a limo."

"I can tell."

"Where are we going?"

"It's a surprise."

"I'm feeling a bit underdressed for the occasion."

You look perfect. "Don't worry, what you're wearing is fine for where we're going," he said, grabbing my hand. "I promise." *I just hope she likes sushi.*

Luckily for him, I did like sushi. As the limo weaved through the streets of Manhattan, I scrolled through the mental list of all the sushi restaurants that I knew of in the city, trying to guess where he was taking me. With no help from his thoughts either, I might add.

I listened to him as he told me more about the role he played within his father's company.

"Basically I do what he wants, when he wants me to do it, and go to the meetings that he doesn't want to attend. It's nice because no one ever asks me any questions since I'm the boss' son," he said, sounding indifferent. "Sometimes I think he has me doing all of this just to keep an eye on his employees."

"Why don't you leave?" I asked after a moment.

And go where? "It's not that easy," he said simply as the limo came to a stop. Then his mood perked up. He smiled and said, "We're here."

FOURTEEN

Our limo was parked outside of the entrance to Le Capitano Hotel—one of the finest and oldest hotels in New York. From the mental list of restaurants that I'd composed earlier in the car, I knew right away that we were eating at Izumi, a high end—and hard to get into—sushi restaurant.

Izumi, located at the top of Le Capitano Hotel, overlooked Central Park and was like an exclusive club where you had to know someone to get a table. At least that's what I'd heard from a co-worker who had tried to bring his wife here a few years ago. Last I heard they were still on the waiting list.

"Izumi?" I said eagerly as we stepped out of the limo, my hand in his.

"You've been here?"

I had to catch myself from doing a small pathetic smile, so instead I said, "No, I've just heard about it from others." After a moment, I asked, "How did you get a reservation on such short notice? I know people who have been waiting over two years for a table."

"I know people." *Wow, way to sound like a douche.*

I slipped my arm through his extended elbow before we walked up the steps to the entrance where a respectable looking doorman stood.

"Hello, Tom," Mark said politely.

"Good evening, Mr. Madison." Tom nodded his head toward us as he opened the door. He looked at me and said, "Ma'am."

Thank God he's not with Nate tonight, I heard Tom as we passed.

"Do you come here a lot?" I asked.

"Nate's father owns the building and is one of the investors of Izumi. So, yes, we've been here a few times."

"A few times... You're on a first-name basis with the doorman."

"Yes, and the bartender and I play poker together." He smirked. "Let's get going. I may know people, but they'll still give my table away."

We walked through the luxurious lobby—although even the word luxurious was an understatement with its tall, gilded pillars, gleaming mosaic floor, and marigold colored walls. There were three decadent crystal chandeliers hanging from the ceiling, placed intricately between the entrance and the elevators at the opposite end of the corridor. Tall ficus plants in vintage blue floral vases occupied the spaces between each column.

I was in awe of the lobby and wondered briefly what the rooms looked like if this was how the lobby was decorated.

"This place is beautiful," I said before we reached the elevators.

"It is nice," he began. "When they purchased the building, it was run down and there was talk of tearing it down completely and building something more modern. One of the architects found out that the building dated back to the late 1800s, so it was restored instead."

"That's great! I wish more old buildings were restored instead of torn down. It's living history!"

"Sometimes tearing them down is necessary."

"Sometimes, but not every time," I insisted. "Places like this just need someone who is willing to put a little extra tender love and care… and some good ol' elbow grease."

He grinned at me, thinking, *Is that all, Texas, good ol' elbow grease?*

A little too late, I answered his thought, "Not that again."

"What's that?" he said as the elevator finally arrived.

"Nothing, just saying again how nice the lobby looks."

The elevator rushed us to the top of the building where we were greeted by a young girl in formal black attire. She showed us to our table by one of the walls of glass that overlooked Central Park. While Izumi's style lacked the grandeur that the lobby held, it had a modern romantic appeal to it. The wood floors and tiled ceiling were colored black, and the walls were painted a dark crimson red. The tables and chairs were all covered in black tablecloths and upholstery, while the table settings matched the red walls.

Once seated, we were approached by a stubby guy, also dressed all in black.

"Hi, my name is Stephen. I will be your waiter this evening. What drinks are we thinking about having tonight?"

Mark looked at me, urging me to order first. I asked, "Can I get a small hot sake?"

Perfect. "Make that a large, please," Mark said with a grin.

Stephen nodded and asked. "Can I get any starters for you?"

Once again, Mark looked at me, and I heard, *Please don't be one of those picky girls that only wants cooked food.*

I closed my menu and said in earnest, "You order. I'll eat anything."

He seemed delighted. *Wow. I'm impressed and I hope she's not joking.* "Tell Renny to make me whatever he's in the mood to prepare," Mark said, at which Stephen nodded and walked away.

At first, I felt uncomfortable and out of place, which Mark noticed, but thanks to his easy demeanor and the drinks, I began to feel more at ease as the night went on. Conversation came easy with Mark, and I figured out that if I let him do most of the talking, hearing his thoughts never became an issue.

Three sushi rolls and two more large hot sakes later, I'd forgotten the fancy restaurant that I was in and the fact that I was on a first date with the very handsome and very out-of-my-league Mark Madison. Instead, it was just him and me, enjoying each other's company and having a fun time—which I was glad to know of for a fact, thanks to his thoughts.

"You've literally been everywhere and you're only thirty-two! I envy you," I said in response to Mark stating he'd been to over thirty countries.

"How could you have made it out of your small town in Texas to only have made it to New York?" he rebutted.

"Well, I've been to London once. With my mom," I said. "We went for a week after I graduated college."

"London is awesome," he said.

"I've just never had the time." I decided to refrain from saying *or the money.* "I was always busy with school," I continued, "and when school was done, I got my big girl job and have stayed busy with that."

"Big girl job?" He laughed.

I laughed too. "Yes."

She's so cute. "I do have to say, Texas," he started, and I rolled my eyes at the nickname before he continued, "I am thoroughly surprised."

"Surprised?"

"How can a tiny thing like you eat the same amount of food as me?"

"A lot of training," I joked, making him chuckle and revealing his dimple. "Let me guess, every other girl you've brought here only eats cooked food?" It felt like a bold move to use his previous thoughts against him.

He lifted an eyebrow and said, "I wouldn't know because I've never brought another girl here." *I wouldn't waste my money on a girl who will only order expensive wine and eat salad.*

I crossed my arms on the table. "You expect me to believe that Mr. Madison has not wined and dined another girl in one of the best restaurants in New York?"

Mr. Madison huh?

My stomach dropped and heat rose through my veins.

"I'm serious," he said finally, gazing seductively at me.

"Can I interest either of you in some dessert tonight?" Stephen interrupted us.

"No thank you," I said. "I couldn't fit another bite, but everything was amazing."

"Same," Mark responded. "Tell Renny he outdid himself. I can take the check when you're ready." *Should I play the whole, you're paying, not me, game? Or is that too cheesy?*

I took my last sip of sake to hide the smile on my face.

Definitely too cheesy.

Mark hopped out of his seat as a tall Japanese man dressed in a white chef's jacket approached our table and shook his hand like an old friend.

"Hey Renny, how are you?" said Mark.

"Valentine's dinner rush is keeping me busy, otherwise great." He smiled at me and then looked back at Mark. "How was your meal?"

"It was wonderful man, thank you so much." Mark gestured to me and said, "Renny this is Riley. Riley this is Renny, the chef and owner of Izumi."

"Nice to meet you." I smiled graciously. "Your place is amazing, and the food was wonderful."

I like this girl, much prettier than the girls Nate brings in here.

"Thank you, and very nice to meet you," he said. "I have to get back to the kitchen, but I just wanted to come say hello. Have a good night."

"You too, Renny."

When he was gone, Mark said, "Speaking of someone who has been all over the world—Renny has some remarkable stories of his own. He studied the art of making sushi in Japan for many years and then ventured to every other country, tasting other foods and learning new techniques before landing here and opening this place."

"That's impressive."

Mark paid the bill, luckily deciding not to play the who's paying game, and we made our way back downstairs. When we were walking out of the lobby, he gently placed his hand on the small of my back, sending shivers up and down my spine.

I want nothing more than to rip this little black dress off right now.

The shivers migrated from my spine to the rest of my body, making me more sensitive to the touch of his hand on my back. I almost wished he'd take me right there in the hotel lobby, but I quickly reminded myself that I wasn't that kind of girl.

The brisk air outside was welcoming to the heat radiating from my body.

We stood there quietly, waiting for the limo, when I realized that it wasn't too far of a walk back to my place if we went through Central Park.

"Could we walk?" I suggested.

Was the limo too much?

"Just a little..." I said a little too late again.

"Just a little what?" he asked suspiciously.

"Oh, just a little chilly outside, but my apartment isn't too far from here." Good save Riley, I thought.

"Okay," he said right as the limo parked. "Let me tell my driver." He walked over and leaned through the window to let his driver know we'd be walking and to pick him up at my apartment—giving no indication of a time to pick him up.

I knew I wouldn't be able to tell him no if I let him come upstairs. I needed to come up with a game plan or a good excuse before we made it back to my place.

I played out several different scenarios in my mind by the time we made it halfway through the park while I half-listened to stories about the adolescent adventures of Mark and Nate. It took me a moment to realize that Mark had asked me a question and was waiting for a response.

"I'm sorry, what?"

"I said, what are you thinking about?" *I guess that story isn't as funny as I thought it was. She looks like she's in another world—or just bored.*

"I'm so sorry," I said again and then lied, "Your story just reminded me of something similar that happened when I was younger."

"Well, go on then. Tell me about it."

Crap. "Oh, no it's not that funny."

"Come on, tell me."

"I promise it's not that good," I answered playfully, hoping he would drop it.

We stopped walking and were facing one another now. Mark studied my face for a moment before slowly moving closer to me and wrapping his arms around my lower back.

I felt the heat of his breath on my forehead and my heart racing in my chest. The musky scent of his cologne invited me to get even closer to him.

Kiss her, dammit.

Before he could make the first move, I slid my hands up his arms toward his face, pulled him closer, and kissed him. He squeezed my waist vigorously, sending pulses through my body from deep within my gut. It seemed as if everything and everyone around us faded away, leaving only him and me there kissing under the stars in Central Park.

What felt like an hour later—but was truly only a minute or less—we broke apart for a breath of air.

He laced his fingers between mine, and we continued walking leisurely in the direction of my apartment again.

"So what was that story you didn't want to tell me?" he asked. *Damn the story, I think I'm going to lose it if I can't have her tonight!*

I know I wasn't supposed to hear him say that, but I found it flattering.

Keep it together, Riley, I thought to myself. You're not that kind of girl, and you're not about to become that kind of girl tonight. "I've already forgotten," I said.

With every scenario that I'd played out in my head earlier now gone out the window, I decided that I was going to let him down outside of my apartment.

Once there, I reluctantly released his hand and began with, "Look Mark—"

Here we go. The I'm-not-that-kind-of-girl talk. They all say that right before they show just how much they are that kind of girl.

I paused, thinking of something else I could say to throw him off. I gave the biggest and most sincere smile that I could summon, then said, "Tonight has been wonderful. Thank you for taking me out."

"Oh." He looked surprised. "You're very welcome." He quickly glanced from me to the door at the top of the stairs leading to my place and back to me.

I looked him in the eyes for a moment, took a deep breath, and quickly made a decision that I hoped wouldn't ruin everything.

***

"I kissed him on the cheek, said goodnight, and went up the stairs before he could say anything else. He was completely speechless, Ashley!" I finished recounting my night with Mark to Ashley later that evening as we sat in our pajamas in the living room.

Ashley was dying with laughter and asked, "He didn't say a word at all?"

"Nope," I said, laughing with her, "not even a thought was uttered."

"Poor Mark! I cannot believe you just left him like that," she said in between giggles. "Why didn't you want to invite him up here?"

"Because I'm not that type of girl!"

"Every girl is that kind of girl after a date like that, Riley."

I rolled my eyes disapprovingly. "Maybe you are, but not me."

Mhmm. She laughed again, then added, "Well, I'm glad that you enjoyed your date." Ashley readjusted herself on the couch to sit up straighter, and looking excited, she said, "My turn now! I met someone at the gym today."

I could tell that she'd been dying to tell me all about the new mystery man. "Oh yeah? Tell me about him."

"I was standing by the water fountain when this tall and *really* good-looking guy that I've never seen at the gym before came up and asked me where the towels were. I showed him but he lingered and told me he was new here—like just moved to the city—and started asking questions about me and the best places to go eat." She paused for a sip of her wine and continued, "We just really hit it off and he asked if he could take me out for coffee sometime this week!"

"That's great! Where is he from?"

"I don't know," she said. "But he is so sexy and very sweet!"

"Okay... What does he do for a living?"

"Uhm, I'm not sure." *If you could've seen the butt on this man...*

I raised one eyebrow at her and smiled.

"What?! Can you blame me? A hot guy approaches me at the gym and asks me out to coffee! I'm excited!"

"I'm just happy that you're happy," I admitted, hoping that this meant the Nate days were behind us. "Did you at least get his name?"

"Duh," she said. "It's Alex."

Fifteen

Mark and I began spending more time together over the next few weeks following our date on Valentine's Day. I was both relieved and surprised to find that dating someone when I could hear their every thought was not as bad as I imagined it would be—although I had my moments.

Overall, I was incredibly happy when Mark and I were together because he was genuinely interested in me and not worried about the prospect of getting laid—something I'd managed to avoid thus far despite the ongoing temptation when we kissed.

Currently, we were waiting for Ashley and her new boyfriend, Alex, to meet us—for the first time—at Johnny's Pub. Since the day they grabbed a coffee together, Ashley had spent all her spare time with him. We'd been trying to plan a double date so I could meet this mystery gym man, but something always came up last minute, causing us to postpone.

I didn't mind because Ashley was happier than she'd been in over a year, and I hadn't heard Nate's name mentioned once since the day she met Alex.

"You still haven't met this guy?" Mark asked as he took a sip of his beer.

"No, I haven't," I said, "but I can tell Ashley really likes him. They've been spending a lot of time together, either at the gym or his place because he works really odd hours supposedly."

"You don't find that strange?" he asked.

"I guess a little, but I don't know," I reasoned. "I think they're just enjoying their time together, and if he works weird hours, it makes sense."

I'm glad she's over Nate. That was pathetic. "If you say so." He wrapped his arm around my shoulders and kissed me lightly on the temple.

"Aww, you two are just the cutest little couple there ever was," came Ashley's voice from behind us. She slid into the booth seat across the table from us, a drink in her hand already.

I looked around, searching for Alex, even though I had no idea what he looked like, but didn't see any sign of him in the bar.

"Hi," I said. "Where's Alex?"

"He couldn't make it. Something with work came up," she replied casually, shrugging her shoulders. "Have you ordered food yet? I'm starving!" *I worked up an appetite before coming here*, Ashley thought.

She smirked at me, knowing that I'd heard her and understood what she meant. I smiled to myself and said, "Yes we did. Onion rings."

I'm beginning to think that guy doesn't actually exist, thought Mark.

"That's too bad. I was looking forward to meeting him," I added.

"Me too," Ashley said. "He has a really strange work schedule and is always on call, it seems."

"What does he do?" Mark's own curiosity was getting the better of him.

Ashley's face twisted in thought. "Something to do with medical equipment repair... like when a machine breaks in a hospital he has to go in or send someone else in to service it. Among other things, I think."

Mark looked impressed. "That sounds interesting." *I can't believe I'm about to even suggest this—Nate's going to kill me...* "Why don't you bring him to my party next weekend?" he suggested.

"Yeah, that'd be great," she answered, excited for a chance to parade her new man around in front of Nate. "Only if you're okay with it since it is your birthday party."

That Nate is planning, they both mimicked one another's thought at the same time.

It was moments like this that I didn't particularly love my ability to hear thoughts.

"Of course," Mark said politely. "The more the merrier."

"Thanks Mark!"

When the onion rings came, Ashley and Mark started arguing about which was better, dipping your onion rings in ketchup or ranch. I let them ramble on, keeping my opinions to myself. My train of thought drifted to several different topics, like how great the last few weeks with Mark had been, the mysterious man named Alex who kept bailing on his girlfriend's best friend, and even thoughts of Ben and what he might be up to in the small town called Logan.

My thoughts stayed on Ben the longest. I wondered what it was like to live for two hundred years, unnoticed by those around you, and I imagined the historical events that he might have witnessed.

Then I wondered how long I might live and the things I would see that everyone else around me in a hundred years would only read about in history books. I hadn't thought about any of this since my drive home from Logan over a month ago because my new reality still felt unreal to me.

Mark's hand squeezed my leg, snapping me out of my thoughts and back to the conversation where Ashley and Mark had agreed to disagree.

"Earlier you said *among other things* when you were talking about what Alex does," I said. "What other things?"

"I'm not really sure, but he's mentioned medical research and something else about rental properties."

"Ash, I don't understand how you could be with someone as much as you have been and still not know anything about them."

"We don't talk much," she responded unapologetically.

Mark coughed into his beer, and I shot her a reproving glance but laughed anyway.

At least someone's getting some, I heard Mark next to me.

"You're ridiculous," I laughed.

She looked at her watch and said, "Speaking of, I need to get going."

"Where?"

"Back to Alex's place. He said he'd be done with work around eleven and asked if I'd meet him back there."

"Alright," I said, "see you later."

"Maybe." She winked. "Bye Mark."

"Bye Ashley."

"I don't think Alex is real," Mark said when Ashley was gone.

I giggled. "Why would you think that?"

"He's blown us off what, three, four times now?"

"Are you dying to meet him that bad?" He knew I was kidding with him.

He smiled. "No, but it does seem odd."

I didn't answer him. I just nodded and rested my head on his arm.

"Are you ready to go, Texas?"

After the first week of dating, I'd accepted his nickname for me, considering it to be more endearing than anything. "Yes," I said, gently stroking the soft hairs on his arm.

I watched Mark in admiration while he waited at the bar to pay our bill. He was making friendly conversation with another person sitting at the bar, something he was good at. He could make friends anywhere he went. His green t-shirt stretched across his broad shoulders, the small dimple poking through the stubble on his cheek when he smiled. Butterflies fluttered around my stomach, and I thought that even though he didn't know what I really was, I felt normal again when I was with him, as if the other part of me didn't exist.

I made my decision right there that I wasn't ready for the night to end yet. I grabbed his black jacket from the booth and met him by the bar when he finished. We didn't speak on the short walk from the bar back to my place.

He turned me around to face him at the bottom of my stoop and kissed me tenderly and slowly. "Well, goodnight then," he murmured as he backed away to leave.

I pulled him back to me and kissed him again, whispering in between, "Would you like to come upstairs?"

His walnut colored eyes widened, and I heard, *Is she being serious? Like upstairs, upstairs?*

I smiled despite knowing I shouldn't have heard that and nodded.

He waited, still unsure if I was being serious, so I grabbed his hand and led the way up the stairs to my apartment.

My heart was pounding in my ears, and I wondered why I was so nervous. It wasn't like I was a virgin or anything—although it had been at least a year since the last time I'd slept with anyone, and last time I couldn't hear what they were thinking the entire time.

I built up every possible bad outcome in my head. What if he judges me? What if he's not enjoying it? What if he's thinking of someone else? All of these I knew were completely ridiculous—he was a guy and guys liked sex.

It was dark in the apartment except for one lamp we had left on in the living room. In my room, I turned the radio on—a quick thought on my part—where "Candle in the Wind" was playing.

For a while, Mark kissed me slowly and discarded one piece of clothing at a time from each of us, making sure to take his time. Between the radio playing in the background and his gentle touch caressing every inch of my skin, if he did have any negative thoughts, I didn't hear them.

That was amazing, he uttered to himself later as we laid there in my bed, still entangled and breathing heavily.

He wasn't wrong, and every negative notion I'd formed in my head about this moment was dispelled immediately. He was resting his head on my bare chest while I stroked his hair.

After catching his breath, he started kissing me on my chest, working his way slowly up my neck to my ear, sending tingly vibrations through my veins until our lips met. We made love again before falling asleep. The last thing I remembered was an Aerosmith song playing on the radio.

***

I woke up earlier than usual the next morning, relieved about last night going better than expected and happy to see Mark still lying beside me, sleeping peacefully. The covers were a tangled mess, leaving one of his butt cheeks exposed.

I snuck out of bed, threw on whatever clothes I could find, and tiptoed to the kitchen to make a pot of coffee.

Ashley's bedroom door was closed, and I wondered if she ever came back home last night.

I had enough time to brush my teeth and tame my morning hair before the coffee finished brewing. I poured two cups and almost made it back to my bedroom door when I heard Ashley's door open.

Well, well, well... Two cups of coffee this morning? Are you doubling up on your caffeine, or do you have a visitor? Ashley was standing in her doorway with the biggest grin on her face, and I couldn't help but smile back, blushing.

"Good for you, girl!" she whispered loudly. "It's about time."

"It's about time?" I laughed. "We've only been seeing each other for a couple of weeks, you hussy."

"Yeah, yeah." *Miss virgin Mary over here, aren't you.*

I shook my head as I walked back to my room.

I heard her shouting inwardly at me right before I was out of earshot, *You can tell me all about it later!*

Mark was still lying where I'd left him, except I was slightly disappointed to see that he had covered up. I didn't know what to do or how long he might sleep. I wished I could've laid there with him all day, but I knew that I would have to get ready for work soon. I sat next to him with my back leaning up against the headboard and grabbed *An American Killing* off my nightstand.

Before I could open the book, Mark reached up and yanked my book from my hands and chucked it behind him. *Oh no you don't!*

He pulled me down onto my back and propped himself up on his arm, positioning himself over me. He still looked half asleep, but he had a grin on his face nonetheless. He bent down and pecked my forehead and then my lips.

"Good morning," he said.

"Good morning to you too," I said while he continued kissing me.

Why the hell is she wearing a shirt? He didn't let that stop him from sliding his hands underneath my shirt.

"I brought you some coffee," I offered meekly.

He eyed me up and down and said, "It can wait."

Sixteen

The rays of the morning light were shining in through my window and bouncing off his stomach muscles. I watched as Mark took the first sip from his coffee cup and set it back down on the table.

Sex in the morning and coffee in bed?! I may never leave. "I thought you'd run out on me this morning," he joked.

"You do realize this is my house, right? It would be kind of hard to run out on *you*." I smiled. "Last night was... nice," I added awkwardly.

More than nice. "Yes, it was... nice."

"I've been wanting to ask you," I started.

"Yeah?"

"What do you want for your birthday next week?"

You. "You."

"I'm serious!"

So am I. "So am I." He grinned ear to ear. "Honestly, I don't need anything." He saw that I wasn't going to accept this answer, then added, "What if you just buy me a drink?"

I rolled my eyes but surrendered, saying, "I think I can manage that." I set my empty cup of coffee down and crawled on top of him. "Sadly, I need to start getting ready for work." I kissed him on the nose and moved off the bed.

Does that mean she wants me to leave?

"You can hang around if you want," I offered, reading his mind and not wanting him to leave.

"Okay," he said, "I can give you a ride to work. It's on my way home."

"Sounds great." I put my t-shirt and shorts on for the second time that morning. "Do you want more coffee while you wait?"

"Sure, but I can grab it." He started to get out of bed in search of his boxers, but I heard Ashley making noises in the kitchen.

I pointed my thumb behind me toward the kitchen and said, "I wouldn't do that if I were you."

"Ashley's here?"

"Yes."

He handed me his cup, slipped his boxers on, and laid back down in my bed.

Ashley was in the bathroom when I went out there, allowing me to avoid another interrogation for now. I quickly filled his mug and brought it back to him. He was analyzing the book he had tossed across the room earlier.

"Do you like this so far? I've heard good things about it."

"I just started it the other day, but so far so good," I said while I perused my closet, looking for something to wear.

I grabbed a sleeveless blue silk top and my dark pencil skirt. After slipping into those, I freshened up my mascara in the mirror. Then I put on some lip gloss and the necklace that my parents had bought me for Christmas a few years ago—a small sterling silver sand dollar with the letter R in the middle.

As I reached for my black button-down blazer, Mark asked, "If you're into murder mysteries, does that mean that you know how to hide a body?"

"Yes, I do. So don't mess with me. Unless you're trying to get rid of Nate, then I'll be glad to help."

He laughed but didn't say anything.

"You ready to go?" I asked.

"What? You're done getting ready? It's only been like fifteen minutes." He sounded surprised. *I thought I had at least an hour!* He jumped out of the bed and hastily got dressed.

"It's alright, you don't have to rush."

He looked irresistible standing there with nothing but his jeans on.

"One second," I said in the middle of him trying to put his shirt back on.

He looked puzzled until I pushed him back down on the bed and straddled him as best I could in my skirt. I dug my fingers in his bare back as I kissed him, only to be interrupted by Ashley knocking on my door.

"Let's go lovebirds, we're going to be late!" she shouted through the door.

"Seriously?" I said to her as we exited my room.

"If I wouldn't have interrupted, would you two have stopped what you were doing in there? You're welcome for making sure you don't incur the wrath of Fred."

She has a point. Although, who's Fred? "She's got a point," Mark muttered half his thoughts. "I offered to give Riley a ride to work. Do you need one too?" Mark asked politely.

What a man, she thought. "That's okay. I have to run an errand on the way," she said. "But thanks." *You two have fun,* she added to me as an afterthought.

Mark's town car was waiting downstairs for us, making me wonder if the driver had waited there all night.

Reading my mind, Mark said, "I paged him when you were refilling my coffee."

"Oh," I said, feeling relieved for the driver.

Mark opened the door for me, allowing me to slide in first. As the car pulled into the road, I asked, "Aren't you going to be late for work?"

"Yes, but there are some perks to being the boss' son. I can be late occasionally," he said, placing his hand on my leg while he gazed out the window. He glanced back at me and added, "Plus, they had a big meeting with our office in China this morning that I didn't need to be there for, so it's more likely that no one will even notice my absence."

Must be nice, I thought to myself.

I grabbed his hand that was resting on my leg and laced my fingers between his, my thoughts drifting back to last night once again. I also wondered if it was possible that being in a relationship could actually work, or did it only work with Mark because hearing his thoughts was tolerable?

I didn't have much time to think before we pulled up in front of Greenhouse Inc.

Mark walked me to the door and kissed me goodbye. Before leaving, he said, "Last night really was amazing."

"It was, wasn't it," I said smiling. "Bye."

Ashley came into my office as soon as she arrived and closed the door as soon as she arrived at work.

Well, spill! she demanded internally.

"Right now?"

"No time like the present!"

"Okay," I said, and began to share the details from the night before, carefully omitting the more intimate anecdotes. I ended the story by saying, "Ash, it was better than I expected. I haven't felt this way about someone in a long time."

"Riley's in loooove," she sang like a child.

"I wouldn't say that I'm in love, but I do really like being around him. It's almost like it's too good. Do you know what I mean?"

"No. I think you're in love," she declared. "Which isn't a bad thing." After a moment, she thought, *So hearing his thoughts wasn't an issue, you know, in bed?*

"Surprisingly no. I guess I should've known that guys aren't really thinking about much... in the moment."

Ashley laughed aloud in agreement.

"I was really nervous at first—to the point that I wasn't sure if I could go through with it—"

Ashley laughed again, this time at me.

"—I'm serious! It was nerve-wrecking!"

"I'm sure it was," she said. "I'm not sure how I'd feel about hearing my lover's thoughts either."

"Moving on," I said. I wanted to change the subject before she could ask any more questions. "How was the rest of your night with Alex?"

"Fine," she said with a smug grin on her face. "He wanted me to tell you that he was sorry for having to bail again."

"All good. We'll meet sooner or later, I'm sure. You two seem to be hitting it off, too."

"We are; he's great," she assured me.

I checked the time on my watch to see how long I had until my meeting with Fly Ways. "We have an hour and a half before the meeting with Fly Ways," I told Ashley.

"Damn, that's today?"

"Yes, can you get me your notes that you were working on last week? And tell Tyler to come back in here with you so we can brief."

"Yes boss," she said sarcastically. "Be right back."

It was difficult to keep images of last night out of my head as Ashley, Tyler, and I sat there discussing strategies for our upcoming meeting. I did my best to stay focused because if today's meeting with Fly Ways went well, it would be the biggest account that my team and I would have acquired in the two years that I'd been running it.

Fly Ways was an up-and-coming airline company that had its start as a private regional airline, catering to wealthy consumers in the Midwest. Last year, the CEO, Tate Donivan, purchased a fleet of commercial planes and was looking for a new marketing agency to help him break out in the full-service airline industry, starting in New York.

My team had been battling for the account against another agency across town for the past six months, and today I expected them to make a final decision—mainly because I wasn't going to let this drag out any longer. My team had been working long hours on an account that wasn't officially ours, and personally, I believed that we were better suited for the job than the other agency.

I also had something that I was sure the other agency did not; I could hear their thoughts.

In our previous meetings, I was able to figure out what the other agency was offering them, and I was confident—because of this knowledge—that we had a better pitch. In addition, Tate and his team were impressed by my ability to respond to their expectations and concerns before they were able to voice them.

At first, it felt unfair to use this ace up my sleeve in order to further my career, but as Ashley so willingly pointed out one evening after I voiced my concerns, no one knew what I was doing or how I was doing it, nor would anyone believe me if I'd told them. Of course, having the knowledge that you can't get caught doesn't make it right. However, I felt justified knowing that I wasn't harming anyone.

Instead of feeling hindered by this gift, I retrained myself to think of it as another tool in my arsenal when necessary.

You're glowing, you know?

Ashley's thought snapped me out of my own as she and Tyler were leaving my office.

I noticed she was grinning at me. When Tyler made it back to his desk, she whispered, "It's a good thing—to be glowing. You've got this!"

The second part I knew was referring to our final meeting with Fly Ways. "Thank you," I said.

When it came time for the meeting, I sat on one side of the boardroom table with Ashley and Tyler on each side of me, and for the first time in six months, Fred, my boss, sat in the corner behind us for observation purposes.

Let's hope she doesn't screw this up.

I heard Fred behind me and rolled my eyes, thankful he couldn't see my face.

Tate and his team—which consisted of three other people; his Chief of Marketing, Margot; the Chief Financial Officer, Franklin; and his assistant, Jessica—sat opposite of the three of us.

Tate was someone who I pictured sitting on an island in the Bahamas, sipping liquor from a coconut shell and smoking an expensive cigar rather than sitting here in a boardroom doing business. He dressed as such, too. Today he was wearing a pair of loose khaki pants and a white button-down cotton shirt. Anyone who passed him on the street wouldn't know he was a millionaire, and I think that was how he preferred it.

The meeting began as it always did; laying out the successes and failures of the test ads we'd run since our last meeting, discussing the research on where else we could market, and the costs.

I did most of the talking, with Tyler and Ashley backing me up when needed. After the first thirty minutes, I thought it was going well.

Billboards and radio advertisements... that's what everyone is doing. Should we even mention that the other agency is offering to get us a spot on one of the local news stations or will that give away what they're doing?

This thought came from Jessica, who usually kept quiet but unknowingly gave away a lot more information than the others with her thoughts during these meetings.

Luckily, I was way ahead of the other team's thought processes by now and had one more card to play that we had been working on since the last meeting, something that not even Fred was privy to up until this point.

I looked sideways at Ashley to give her the go ahead.

She started with, "Another method of advertising that we acquired for you last week is airtime on CNN, every hour, all day long."

CNN?! *Where on earth...*

Fred kept his mouth shut but I could hear his thoughts loud and clear behind me. I also noticed the four people across from me shift forward in their seats, waiting for more.

Tyler, knowing it was his turn to proceed, stood up and turned on the small television hanging on the wall. He played a short snippet of a mock commercial for Fly Ways that he'd been working on since we came up with this plan over a month ago.

After it was over, Ashley slid four pieces of paper across the table, showing another mock ad for a newspaper. "We have also procured a quarter of a page in *The New York Times* travel section for at least one year with an opportunity to renew."

I paused, letting this new bit of information sink in for everyone, including Fred.

"Both companies are waiting on the go ahead from me to air your ad campaigns," I said finally, looking directly at Tate, who seemed impressed. "What should I tell them?"

Two hours and sixteen signatures later, my team was celebrating our first big account. Someone had even opened an old bottle of champagne that they found in the breakroom refrigerator. After toasting with them, I went back to my office and left them to celebrate their winnings, while I celebrated my own relief in the silence of my office.

I heard a knock on my door a minute later and looked up to see Fred letting himself in my office.

"That was damn good work in there, Riley," he said truthfully.

"Thank you, sir."

"How were you able to get CNN on board with that?"

"Ashley knows someone over there, and we have been communicating with them for weeks. It took some time, but we finally persuaded them to agree to air time without revealing who the client was going to be," I offered readily. "*The New York Times* was easier to deal with from my connections over there from past advertisement gigs, and Tyler has a friend who is going to school for videography with a minor in graphic design. He was glad to help create the mock commercial for us. It all just came together after that."

"What gave you the idea that they were even interested in that kind of advertising?" he asked.

"It was a shot in the dark, sir," I said untruthfully.

"Hmph," he said. "Well, good work... really good work."

Before he left my office, I heard, *I don't know how she did it. It's like she's a mind reader.*

I smiled to myself and thought if only he knew.

I was on cloud nine between my relationship with Mark and now my disgruntled boss being proud of the work I'd done. I knew I was naive to think it could stay like this forever, but then again, at least for me, forever was possible.

SEVENTEEN

I admired myself one last time in Mark's full-length bathroom mirror. I was wearing my red spaghetti strap dress—the same red dress that Ashley had advised me not to wear on our Valentine's Day date but insisted that it was perfect for Mark's birthday party tonight.

I didn't disagree with her. The sleek fabric flattered my hourglass figure but not in a way that restricted my breathing or movement in any way.

The dress was a classic knee-length style, except for a long slit up the side that almost reached the top of my thigh. I moved my leg around to assess how revealing the dress would be if I shifted one way or the other. It seemed safe enough, so long as I didn't do any high kicks tonight.

It wasn't the kind of dress that I ever thought I'd buy for myself, mostly because the retail price was higher than the rent for my Upper West Side apartment. However, I had a hefty Christmas bonus, and Bloomingdale's had an affordable holiday sale.

After that, the beautiful, overpriced dress hung unemployed in my closet until tonight.

I felt comfortable and confident wearing it, which I thought was a good start to the night that lay ahead of us.

Nate had been planning this party for weeks, which included inviting everyone he and Mark knew and booking a VIP lounge room at a very upscale nightclub called Regal.

There was no expense spared in his planning, and while Mark never said it aloud, he wasn't too thrilled about spending his birthday in a club with a bunch of people he hadn't seen in years—and if I was being honest, neither was I.

He didn't want to let Nate down though. I'd heard him thinking last week that he'd never seen Nate put so much effort into a task before, so he let him proceed without complaint.

I smiled, thinking back to the night that he invited me to come as his date after receiving a call from Nate about several girls who were going to be there.

"You won't go to your own party if I don't go?" I repeated, amused.

"Nope," he said. *I'd rather have her there than all the gold-digging bimbos that Nate has invited.*

"I think you're being a little dramatic," I said.

"Maybe." He smiled, and I waited for another thought to come. Instead, he added, "That doesn't change the fact that I want you there."

I blushed, knowing we had only been seeing each other for a few weeks, but here he was, asking me to go to a party that wasn't for several more weeks.

"Fine," I conceded. "I guess I can pencil it in. But just know that if something better comes up, I'm ditching you."

Knowing that I was joking, he laughed out loud and said, "If something better comes up, we're *both* ditching this party."

Unfortunately, no better plans came up—though we concocted many alternative options in the weeks that followed, making it a game by coming up with things we would rather be doing than go clubbing.

I finished applying my mascara and lip gloss and put on my silver necklace, the one that I always wore with my initial in the middle, along with a pair of small diamond studded earrings.

At the same time, I heard Mark enter his bedroom, saying, "Are you ready? The car is—" he stopped mid-sentence when he saw me, gawking at me for a moment before finishing his sentence, "—here." *Holy shit, she looks sexy. I wonder how pissed Nate would be if I skipped my own party.*

"Yes," I said, smirking to myself. "I just need to put my shoes on."

He came up behind me and ran his hands up my body slowly, starting at my hips.

"You look amazing, Riley."

Chills ran up my spine as his hands made their way to the strap on my dress, where he playfully made it fall off my shoulder.

I giggled and caught it before it could reveal anything. "Thank you," I said, turning around to kiss him, wrapping both of my arms around his neck. "Didn't you say the car was here?" I asked in between kisses.

"Yes, but it can wait. It is *my* birthday after all."

Both his hands were resting on my backside now and when he squeezed tightly, I almost said to hell with his party.

"There's plenty of time for that later," I said, barely convincing myself.

He groaned. "I don't know if I can wait until later." He made the strap on my dress fall again, but this time I didn't catch it. I couldn't resist allowing him to kiss my chest, and I became lost as his warm lips grazed gently across my skin.

Before we could get any further, the front door buzzer rang loudly from the foyer.

Dammit, he thought.

"I told Ashley we would pick her up by 9:30, so we should probably get going anyway," I said, fixing my shoulder strap for the second time.

I completely forgot about that. He looked down at his watch and said, "That's not going to happen. It's already ten minutes till." He studied me for a moment, and I listened to his thoughts as he considered whether we should blow off Ashley and Nate to stay home and rip my dress off or leave and be cockblocked by his own birthday party.

The corner of my mouth twitched, and I stood on my tippy toes to kiss him on the cheek. "Don't worry, I promise you I won't let you go to sleep later on until you finish what you just started."

What a tease! "Alright, let's go," he said with indignation.

More than an hour later, the three of us pulled up to Regal, late and buzzing on champagne. The beat of the music playing inside was resonating through the town car, which was parked outside the front entrance. The line of people waiting to get inside was half a block long, but with Mark being who he was, we were able to walk right inside without any question from the bouncer.

I couldn't help but feel superior as the people waiting in line gaped at us in awe as we passed. I held on tight to Mark, who seemed unfazed by their stares, and noticed Ashley, who was following closely behind us, was enjoying all the attention.

Inside, the air was heavy with smoke and the smell of stale liquor. It was dark except for the flashes of neon lights dancing with the beat of the song playing. I was grateful for the loud music because it meant that I wouldn't be able to hear anyone's thoughts.

We were led to the back of the building and up a staircase to the room that Nate booked for the party. While it was not as loud in the suite, people's thoughts were still muffled by the vibrations from the music.

The room was smaller than I'd imagined, but still roomy. It was rectangular, with two long, leather couches lining two of the walls. On the opposite wall from one of the couches was a wide glass window which overlooked the dance floor below. In between the window and couches were two circular tables and chairs scattered around. Every surface was covered with empty plastic shot glasses and half full drinks.

There were several guys I didn't recognize sitting at the tables and chairs, while Nate and six blonde girls—who all looked alike, and I assumed were the gold-digging bimbos that Mark wanted to avoid—were occupying one of the sofas.

The guys seated at the tables all stood at the same time to greet us when we entered the room, hugging Mark, wishing him happy birthday, and introducing themselves to Ashley and me one by one.

Nate and his groupies didn't notice our presence until we were through the initial group of guys. When he noticed Mark, Nate hopped off the couch, leaving the girls in utter disappointment, and gave Mark a big hug.

"Happy birthday, bro!" Nate shouted over the music. "What do you think?"

I knew he was not talking about the expensive lounge room that he rented, but instead he was referring to the six blondes he'd brought for Mark.

Mark nodded politely and I couldn't tell if he didn't pick up on what Nate actually meant, or if he was just ignoring him. Mark responded, "How do we get drinks up here?"

"There's a mousy little goth girl running back and forth. She should be back up here soon," he said carelessly. "Come meet everyone."

Nate had his arm around Mark's neck still and pulled him toward the couches where the six blondes waited patiently for Nate's return.

He had completely ignored Ashley and me, which didn't bother me—I was confident that Mark wasn't going home with anyone but me—however, I could tell it struck a nerve with Ashley. We stood by the window and watched the people dancing below us.

Ashley kept her eyes on the entrance for any sign of Alex—she assured me that he was actually going to show tonight. I told her I would believe it when I saw him.

I glanced back at Mark and laughed when I saw him mouthing the words 'Help me.'

"Want to go grab a drink down there?" Ashley asked.

"Sure, let me go tell Mark."

I approached Mark, who had a look of relief on his face at the sight of me. He grabbed me by the waist and pulled me close to him.

I spoke into his ear so that I wouldn't have to shout. "Ashley and I are going to go grab a drink downstairs real quick. Can you manage being alone with Nate and the bimbos for a few minutes?"

He laughed, looked from me to Ashley and back, thankfully understanding her need to go downstairs instead of waiting up here for the waitress, and nodded his head up and down.

"Hurry back," he said before kissing me hard on the lips.

I couldn't help but feel elated by the displeased looks on Nate's face, along with two of the girls.

While we waited for our drinks, I shouted to Ashley, "What did you expect?"

She shrugged her shoulders. "Not for him to completely ignore me or have six girls hanging all over him."

"I'm not surprised," I said. "Plus, you have Alex now. So why are you upset? Where is he, by the way?"

"He told me that he was coming later on."

"I'm glad that I finally get to meet him," I yelled.

"You haven't met him yet?!" Ashley looked surprised.

"Uhm, no." I shook my head side to side just in case she didn't hear me.

"When would we have met?" I asked loudly.

She contemplated this as the bartender handed us our drinks. I showed the bartender the stamp on my hand, indicating that we were with Nate's party.

Ashley finally said, "I can't believe you haven't met Alex. For some reason I thought we had hung out once or something."

"You mean that one time we almost met last weekend at Johnny's when he was a no show?"

She unapologetically shrugged her shoulders again. A moment later, Ashley's eyes widened with excitement at someone behind me.

I turned to see a tall, handsome man coming toward us with a smile on his face that dominated the room. People parted the way for him to pass without him having to ask. He was dressed fashionably in all black attire: a black button down, black slacks, and a black leather jacket. The top two buttons of the shirt were unbuttoned, revealing a small cluster of dark chest hair.

Once he was closer, I could see that his features strongly resembled that of an Indian man. His skin was the color of milk chocolate, and his eyes were mahogany brown. I had to admit that he was a very good-looking person, and there was something mesmerizing about his gaze.

Ashley jumped into his arms and kissed him eagerly, as if they were the only two people in the club. I thought it was sweet, and I was happy that she found someone who seemed good for her. Suddenly though, when I caught Alex glancing briefly at me before releasing Ashley, I felt a small stab jealously at the thought of her kissing him, wishing momentarily it was me.

The feeling disappeared as quickly as it came when he looked away from me.

EIGHTEEN

Ashley attempted to introduce us despite the thunderous beat of the music playing. Alex took my outstretched hand and shook it gently.

I leaned in and shouted, "Nice to finally meet you!"

"You as well," he mouthed to me.

I looked at Ashley and gestured back up toward the VIP lounge. Instead, she took her drink from my hand that I'd been holding while she greeted Alex and pointed to the dance floor.

I left them there and headed back to the suite, where Mark greeted me eagerly. I tasted the bitter tang of tequila and lime juice on his lips, and his eyes were slightly glazed over.

I wondered how many shots Nate had given him in my absence.

"Where's Ashley?" he asked.

"Down there." I gestured out the viewing window to the dance floor. "I finally met Alex." I could see them in the middle of the dance floor, grinding on one another to a remixed Outkast song.

"Oh, nice," Mark said.

Mark sat back down by the guy he was talking with when I'd come into the room and gestured for me to sit in the chair next to him where I still had a view of Ashley. Currently, she and Alex were dancing, laughing, and stealing kisses from one another. I couldn't remember the last time that I'd seen her so happy.

"Stephen, have you met my girlfriend, Riley?" Mark said casually.

I turned my attention back to him, my insides burning. He hadn't referred to me as his girlfriend yet.

"No, I don't think we have," Stephen said smiling. "Nice to meet you, Riley."

Stephen looked much younger than all the other guys here tonight, his clean-shaven baby face giving him away—however, I could tell that he was more levelheaded than all of them. He had tanned olive skin with honey-colored curls on top of his head and wore square, wire-rimmed glasses. He seemed out of place compared to the rest of the group.

"Hi," I said. "How do you two know one another?"

"Nate invited him into our poker group after they played in a golf tournament together a few years ago," Mark said. "Right?"

"That's correct," said Stephen. "They haven't been able to get rid of me since then, mostly because I keep taking all of Nate's money in poker, and he's determined to recoup it."

We all laughed, and I joked, "Well, I'm rooting for you to keep winning."

Mark was still smiling. "Don't worry, Nate doesn't have a chance. Stephen is a master poker player."

"I wouldn't say I'm a *master*. I'm just lucky I guess," he said as he winked at me.

"Who's ready for another round?!" Nate shouted right as the waitress was entering the room with a tray full of shots.

"Oh man," Mark mumbled, "you might be carrying me home later."

"I'm alright with that." I squeezed his thigh playfully.

"Here you go, kids," Nate said, handing all three of us a shot.

"Bottoms up, birthday boy," I said, toasting Mark.

The fiery liquid burned as it passed down my throat into my stomach, coating my insides in its cruel fashion. "Gah, that's awful!" I said after a moment.

"It really is," Mark agreed, almost gagging.

"It'd be better if it wasn't cheap tequila." Stephen's face was also pinched with disgust.

"I don't think shooting tequila can ever taste good," I protested.

"Well... you're not wrong. However, I have had some tequila that goes down as smooth as water," he offered. Then he added when he could tell that I wasn't convinced, "But you definitely have to acquire a taste for tequila."

"I know what you mean," I said. "Personally, I enjoy drinking whiskey every once in a while, but most people don't know how I can handle the taste of it."

Both Mark and Stephen looked stunned by my response.

Stephen asked first, "On the rocks or straight?"

"It depends," I answered, and in the hopes of steering the conversation away from me, I asked, "So when is your next poker game?"

"I'm not sure," Mark said, still seeming impressed with me. "We've got that fishing trip in a few weeks though."

"Oh, yeah," Stephen responded, which prompted a long discussion about where they were going, the type of boat they were taking, and who would get seasick first this time.

Mark had told me that the fishing trip had been an annual tradition for him and Nate since they were teenagers. It started as a day trip with their dads on a small charter boat, and over the years turned into a five-day trip on a yacht, still with their dads but now including several of their closest friends.

I looked down to check on Ashley and found her and Alex standing by the bar, waiting on drinks, with her back facing me. I noticed that Alex was staring at me, a sinister look in his eyes. I felt scared and chills ran up and down my spine, but I couldn't make myself look away from him. Despite how warm it was in the room, I could feel the prickly sensation of goosebumps forming on my arms.

Then within seconds, anger spread through me like wildfire, my arms became tense, and I was breathing heavily.

It wasn't until Mark put his arm around me, breaking my eye contact with Alex, that I felt normal again.

"Everything okay, Texas?" he asked.

"Yeah," I uttered, still trying to figure out what the hell had just happened. "Yes, I'm fine."

A few minutes later, Ashley came bouncing into the room, a wide grin on her face.

"Hey!" I said. Then I asked nervously. "Where's Alex?"

"He had to go make a phone call. He said he'd be up in a minute," she explained breathlessly. "I haven't danced this much in years! Isn't he the sexiest man you've ever seen—" she paused, glancing at Mark, who didn't seem to be paying attention or if he was, didn't care, but she said anyway, "—sorry Mark!"

"He's something," I said, trying to sound neutral. There was no denying that he was attractive, but there was something about him that made me wary.

"I need to go to the bathroom. Come with me, please?" Ashley demanded.

"Okay." I was hoping that we would pass Alex in the hallway so I could potentially hear a thought from him and learn more about this mysterious man.

Unfortunately, we never passed Alex, but on our way back we did encounter Nate, who was heavily intoxicated and stumbling on his way to the men's bathroom. He noticed us and walked directly up to Ashley, pushed her up against the wall, and began kissing her sloppily.

I heard him slurring his words to her as he said, "You look so damn hot tonight. And showing up here with another guy is turning me on."

I thought for a second that Ashley was going to allow him to continue with his horrible display of affection. That was until she pushed him away and slapped him as hard as she could across the face.

She yelled, "I didn't come here tonight with my *boyfriend* to make you jealous, asshole! I am here for Mark's birthday and that's it!"

"Come on, I saw the way you were looking at me while grinding up against that loser," he said, completely unfazed by the slap she'd just administered which was turning his pale-colored cheek bright red.

It looked like he was about to fall over, but the wall caught him before he could lean any further.

"Oh please! You're out of your mind if you believe that load of crap!" She crossed her arms. "It seems as if *you* were the one watching *me*. Why don't you just go back to your group of blondes and go to hell! Come on, Riley!"

She turned to leave but he wasn't backing down. Nate grabbed her by the arm and looked as if he was going in for another kiss but pleaded, "Ash please! I want you so bad! I shouldn't have brought them here tonight! All I want is you! Those braindead losers mean nothing to me!"

At the same time, we heard two people gasp behind us. It was two of the girls from the group upstairs who apparently heard everything Nate said as they were exiting the bathroom. One of them walked towards Nate and threw her drink in his face, while the other one slapped him clean across the other cheek. They both stormed off, leaving us all in shock.

Ashley and I left Nate standing there with a vacant expression on his face, laughing as we made our way back toward the suite.

She stopped at the bottom of the staircase and said, "I think I'm going to find Alex and go."

"Are you okay?"

"I am more than okay." She smiled, feeling proud of herself. "I just don't want to chance running into him again."

"I understand," I said. "I'm not going to lie though, that was totally awesome what you did back there."

An even bigger grin spread across her face.

"Are you going home tonight?" I asked.

"Not sure yet. Either way, I'll see you tomorrow as I'm sure you're staying with Mark tonight."

"Yes, I am," I said hugging her. "Be careful."

She hugged me back and headed toward the bar in search of Alex.

Once back in the suite, I first noticed that the group of girls had all left; no doubt the other two came back and told the rest what had happened in the bathroom hallway.

The second thing I noticed was that Alex had taken my seat next to Mark and Stephen, who were still talking about boats when I approached.

To avoid eye contact with Alex, I kept my eyes on the tuft of chest hair sticking out of his shirt and said, "Hey, Ashley went back to the bar looking for you. I think she's ready to leave."

"I guess I should go find her then." He stood to leave, an odd feeling of lust beginning to take over me, but this time I fought it. Before finally leaving, he said, "Gentlemen, Riley, nice to meet all of you."

"You too," we all said at the same time.

"That was strange, right?" I asked Mark when he was gone.

"What was? The way he was checking you out?" He put both arms around my waist and said, "Can you blame him? I know I couldn't take my eyes off you all night." He kissed my forehead and added softly in my ear, "I'm ready to go home and get this dress off of you."

"That sounds great." I pulled him closer and kissed him hard, not caring about the last few people who remained in the room.

Back outside, the cool crisp air was welcoming after breathing the heavy club air for the last few hours. Even the regular noises of traffic and people talking was a relief to the pounding of the music that still rang in my ears.

Once we were in the car, I filled Mark in on the drama that ensued between Nate and Ashley.

"I wondered why they all left in such a hurry," he said amused.

"May I ask why you are friends with him?"

"Despite how he treats women, which I know makes him look like a complete ass, he is a really good friend."

"Mhmm," I said, "I'm sorry to say this, but you should've seen the look on his face after the second slap. Although, he was so drunk that I wouldn't be surprised if he forgets about both slaps."

Mark chuckled. *He wouldn't care anyway. He's most likely already found another girl to bring home by now.*

Since I couldn't comment on this aloud, I asked, "How about you... How was your night?"

"It was great. I'm happy that I got to catch up with a few of those guys." *Hopefully, the night is about to get a lot better though.*

At this thought, I crawled on top of him, started unbuttoning his shirt and kissed his neck slowly. He pulled my hips closer to him, making my dress slide above my hips.

I was thankful that there was a privacy partition between us and the driver.

"I want you right now," he breathed in my ear, and for the third time tonight, pulled the strap of my dress off my shoulder, his lips caressing my bare chest.

Knowing that we didn't have enough time to make love because we would be back at his apartment soon, I slid onto the floor instead and unzipped his pants.

Hell yeah!

It was all I heard from him until we arrived—with perfect timing—at his place, several minutes later. We had just enough time to put ourselves back together before the driver opened the door to let us out.

We walked hand in hand through the white marbled lobby, a smile lingering on both of our faces. The elevator ride felt much longer than usual because there were other people riding up with us, and we had to contain the sexual tension we had built up.

Once the elevator doors opened to Mark's floor, the gentleman in him stayed behind while an excited boy took over, removing all our clothes hastily and without effort. He kissed me intensely for several minutes before lifting me into his arms and carrying me to the bedroom, pinning me against the cold wall at one point.

He laid me on his bed a moment later, and I attempted to remove my heels.

He grabbed my hand, and with a mischievous grin on his face said, "Leave them."

***

It was almost two o'clock in the morning when I left Mark lying on the bedroom floor, wrapped in his bed covers and sleeping like a baby. Physically, I was exhausted, but mentally, my mind was restless, making it hard to sleep.

I threw on the first shirt that I could find and went into the kitchen to pour myself a glass of water. I opened the sliding glass door to Mark's balcony, which offered an amazing view of the city below. It was windy up here, but I found it refreshing as I became lost in my own thoughts.

Mark turned thirty-two yesterday, and he didn't look any different than thirty-one. I thought, as I had many times before, when did a person start looking older? Do people take a good hard look at themselves every ten years and realize how much has changed or how much they've changed? I know how much I changed between the ages of twenty and thirty, but I still found it hard to believe that I'd still look the same at forty as I do now. How long would it take people to notice?

And what about my mind? Ben said he was over two hundred years old, but if I didn't know that, I would have believed he was in his mid-thirties by the way he acted. Plus, he told me the other guy, Odin, was over a thousand years old. I'd never met him, but I pictured him having a hunched back with a long white beard and an old wooden cane. However, Ben talked about him as if he were a brother.

I thought that I'd have to ask Ben the next time I talked to him—whenever that might be. I hadn't heard from him, nor had I tried to call him since I left Logan over two months ago.

I was finally beginning to feel drowsy, so I made my way back inside and laid down next to Mark on the floor. I rested my head in the crook of his shoulder and was running my fingers over his chest when he pulled me closer and kissed me softly on the forehead.

Nineteen

Three weeks later...

I was woken up abruptly by the sound of wind rushing through the room and a bright, golden-white glow surrounding the face of a person that I didn't know. The person uttered the familiar phrase that I'd heard all those months ago...

> *Thomas Lancaster is no longer with us.*
> *Their ability has passed on to Lin Cho.*

It was exactly like the first dream—or vision—except this time it was a small and muscular man. He had a smooth, round face with a military buzz cut. His small beady eyes stared directly into mine before vanishing.

Of course, knowing what I knew now, this was Thomas Lancaster, just as the other woman was Joanna Glasgow. I also knew this appearance meant that another one of us was dead.

I rolled over in my bed and saw that it was 1:31 in the morning. Too early to wake Ashley up and tell her about this, but then again, I remembered that I still never told her about the first one, nor what they meant.

I hated that she still didn't know anything beyond the fact that I could hear people's thoughts because I desperately wanted to talk to someone about all of it. However, I still didn't feel right divulging not only my secret but nine other people's secret as well.

Since the night of Mark's birthday, I'd considered telling him about me, but things were going so well between us that I didn't want to risk screwing it up. Surprisingly, Ashley agreed with this sentiment as well.

We'd been spending a lot more time together and I'd even heard him thinking about telling me he loved me one night. That was more disturbing than anything I'd learned about myself since this life-altering change. I had the same thought over and over again since hearing it; how could he love someone he barely knew?

Maybe because he doesn't know that he barely knows who you are, my thoughts came loud and clear.

There was always Ben. I didn't know if it would be strange to call him up out the blue after all this time, but he was the only person I knew who shared the same problems as me. I was sure that we were all thinking the same thing—three deaths in four months. Even I knew that this wasn't normal for people like us.

I fell back asleep shortly after deciding that I would call Ben in the morning.

I was waiting on Ashley to leave for her typical Sunday morning errands before calling Ben. Normally, she left early to go to the gym and then did her weekly grocery shopping afterwards. However, this morning, of all mornings, she was in the kitchen cooking French toast when I came out of my room.

"There's a full pot of coffee," she said cheerily.

"Someone's in a good mood this morning," I said. "Aren't you usually out at the gym or the grocery?"

"Yes, but I'm going to see Alex for a while before he leaves town this afternoon. I figured I'd hit the gym and grocery store later."

"Oh," I said quietly.

I never told Ashley about the strange feelings that came over me when Alex was around at Mark's party. Luckily, I had not seen him again since that night, and she never mentioned anything weird happening with him, so I chalked it up to bad booze. Though I was still curious about him.

I asked casually, "Where is he going?"

"He called me this morning to say that there was some work emergency back in Houston that he had to go deal with for a couple of days." She flipped French toast onto two plates for me and her. "He wasn't sure when he'd be back, so I told him that I'd come by after breakfast to bid him farewell." *If you know what I mean.*

"Ashley, I *always* know what you mean." I laughed and took the plate from her. "I don't know what I'd do without you and your amazing French toast, roomie."

She beamed a smile at me with a mouthful of syrupy toast and mumbled, "What are you up to today?"

"I'm not sure. Maybe just catch upon some reading or work a little."

"Boring!" She swallowed her bite and asked, "Is Mark still gone?"

"Yes."

Mark was away for the weekend on their annual fishing trip. He and fifteen other guys left on Friday and were supposed to be coming back today, but he informed me that sometimes they ended up staying out there until Monday or Tuesday if the fishing was good.

"When does he get back?" Ashley asked.

"I'm not really sure. Could be today or Tuesday apparently," I responded indifferently. "I'm not going to lie, it's been nice having some alone time."

"Mhmm!" she hummed in agreement. *I'm looking forward to having a few days off from the love making myself.*

"Too much information!" I shouted and laughed at the same time.

She laughed too, almost spitting her food out of her mouth. "Oops! I didn't mean for you to hear *that.*"

"Do the two of you ever just hangout, or is it all sex?" I wasn't sure why I asked because I didn't really want to know.

"What do you mean? We watch movies—" *But always miss the endings.* "Well, we've gone for walks in the park—" *But then there were those couple of times that we did it behind the bushes or under Eaglevale Bridge.*

"Okay! I see your point," she surrendered. "Is it such a terrible thing? He's hot and an excellent lover—stop laughing! You and Mark can't keep your hands off one another either!"

"You're right, but at least we finish the movies that we're watching or wait until we get home instead of sneaking into the bushes."

"Whatever." She tried to hide the smile on her face but failed.

"You go get ready," I offered when we were done eating. "I'll get the dishes. Thanks for breakfast!"

You're welcome! I heard as she headed to her room to change.

After she left, I sifted through the papers on my desk and found the small piece of paper containing Ben's phone number. I couldn't help but feel nervous as I sat down on the couch and dialed.

"Hello, this is Ben," the deep familiar voice said after a few rings, making my heart sink into my stomach.

"Hey Ben," I started awkwardly. "It's Riley. Riley Bandoni."

"Riley! Hey! How have you been?"

"I've been good. How about you?"

"Same as usual. Nothing has changed here in Logan." He paused and then added, "I assume you're calling about the vision last night."

"Well—yes, and to catch up," I added hastily, not wanting to seem as if I only called when I needed him, even though that's exactly what I was doing. "I'm sorry that I haven't called sooner. I've been busy with work and whatnot."

"No need to apologize to me. I get it," he said. "As far as the vision goes..."

I waited for him to continue, and when he didn't, I began, "I know I'm new to all of this, but isn't it strange? Three deaths in four months?" I winced at saying the word 'deaths' aloud.

"Yes, it is. I don't know what to think of it. In all my years, I've never had three visions this close together. Even Odin—the one who's been around longer than any of us—has never experienced this either. He called me first thing this morning and we agreed that something is going on."

He paused, and neither of us said anything for a minute. Then he added to try and sound reassuring, "It could be nothing, too. I mean, I don't want to sound like I'm brushing off their deaths—Peter, Joanna, and Tommy were great people, and I'm sorry to lose them—but we have no idea if their deaths were an accident or not. Odin told me that he and Elliot were going to try and track down their last whereabouts and get some more information on their deaths."

"Yeah," I answered absentmindedly, wanting to believe him but unsure that it was pure coincidence. I finally replied, needing to say more, "If there is anything I can do to help, please let me know. I didn't know these people, but we have to stick together, right?"

He laughed a little. "Right. Don't worry, I'll keep you posted as soon as I hear anything."

"Thanks," I said. "How's Staci?"

"She's great. Sharp as usual," he replied. "She told me the other day that she wants to take a few business classes on the side, that way she'll feel better taking over for me when I kick the bucket—her words, not mine."

We both laughed out loud, the irony not lost on either of us.

"Good for her for being ambitious I guess."

"What about you? How have you been... adjusting?"

"It's gotten easier," I said. "I've actually been using it to my advantage at work and landed a big account a couple of weeks ago because they liked that I could *read their minds.* Although, I still can't ride the subway."

He chuckled before saying, "I can see that. Does anyone else know other than your roommate?"

"No. Still just her, and she only knows about me."

I didn't want the conversation with Ben to end yet. It was nice having someone who I didn't have to hide anything about myself from, someone who understood better what I was going through than anyone.

I asked, "Any festivals going on in the town right now?"

"Yes, actually," he said, not sounding in a rush to get off the phone either. "This coming weekend is our Founder's Day Festival."

"Founder's Day? Like the day the town was founded? As in, you celebrate the day *you* started the town?"

"I know, it sounds odd, but it wasn't my idea to begin with." I could tell Ben was smiling, and I pictured his bearded grin on the other side of the phone. "To be fair, no one knows that I was there the day we broke ground on the town."

"Broke ground?" I repeated.

"Well, that's how the town tells the story; that our forefathers broke ground on several of the buildings at once and that one of the men named the town after their son, and that's how Logan started."

"Is that true?" I asked.

"Kind of, but not really. After the first ten years or so, we established a pretty sizeable community, going from fourteen people to well over a hundred," he reminisced. "I remember gathering with everyone over several long days to eat, drink, and dance—a toast to prosperity. Every year since then, the people of Logan continued to get together and celebrate."

"Wow."

"Yeah," he agreed. "Eventually it became the Founder's Day Festival and consists of the same things as the first one did—eating, drinking and dancing—but in a more modern fashion."

"You're a living time machine!"

He huffed in amusement. "I've never heard that one before."

"Seriously! To be honest, I still find this whole not aging thing hard to believe. Knowing that there are people out there who have lived through historic events or that I might live through historic events that have yet to come." I hadn't been able to talk about this with anyone since Ben told me about it.

"I get it. It *is* a bit unbelievable. Wait till you hear some of Odin's stories—he used to be a Viking."

"What?!"

"Yeah. Craziest stories you'll ever hear, and it's nothing like reading about it in the books."

"I'm sure," I replied, still trying to picture this Odin guy—who I still pictured as an old man, bent over a cane, with a beard trailing the ground. Now I pictured what I'd only read about in stories—a burly man, over six feet tall, with wild hair braided into a ponytail. Someone who wore animal skins as clothing and looted for a living.

Once all the images of what Odin potentially looked like passed through my mind, I asked, "And the name Logan?"

"That part they have right," he said coolly. "Logan was my son."

I instantly regretted asking the question, having brought up what must have been unhappy memories. I was at a loss for how to respond.

Thankfully he noticed and responded first, saying, "It's okay. Don't feel bad. He passed away peacefully and at an old age a long time ago."

"I'm sorry, I didn't mean to bring up—well, I guess I never thought..." I trailed off, not sure how to say what I was thinking.

"That someone like us had kids?" he asked, finishing my train of thoughts for me. "I had two kids actually, and a wife, before my change happened," he continued, willingly telling me his story. "My wife and daughter—Annie and Hannah—both died young. Then it was just Logan and me. We traveled all around the Americas during a time when it was still wild, and we fought side by side in wars."

I asked cautiously, "When did you know something was different about you?"

"The extra strength was a little odd, but it's definitely one of the more subtle abilities between all of us. After a while it became normal. The not aging was a different story." He paused to laugh at himself from a memory he was picturing. "There was this one time during one of the wars we were fighting in, me and a couple of the guys were sitting around a fire one night and someone asked me how I liked fighting alongside my father—talking about Logan."

"Oh my gosh!" I laughed along with him. "What did he do?"

"Logan was infuriated but he played along, not wanting to draw attention to us if people realized that I was supposed to be older than him."

"Poor Logan," I teased.

He chuckled. "Yeah, but it did make us realize there was something more to my strength. I should've been pushing eighty or ninety by then, and he was the one graying out." He paused before saying, "His last words to me were, if I refused to die, the least I could do was continue to live a life worth remembering. Which is exactly what I did."

I thought to myself how depressing it must have been to watch everyone you love die while you stay the same. When you know you have a short amount of time on this Earth to live, it gives you motivation to be the best you can be. Being immortal can almost make you feel like a failure if you're not always living life to its fullest potential, no matter how long you get to try.

I finally said, "That must have been hard."

"It was for a time, but I have no regrets—I can't, or I'll get stuck. The people of the town have become my family and my purpose for being here," he said proudly. "And of course the others. I've told you before that when I finally met Odin and he explained everything to me, I didn't feel alone anymore."

I started thinking about all the people that I'd lose eventually, my mom and dad, sister, her unborn child, my brother, Ashley, and Mark. I wondered if I'd ever be able to come to terms with their losses.

"Look, don't beat yourself up about the future," Ben said, reading my mind. "I've seen it drive some of the sanest people mad. I can't tell you how many times I've thought 'why me' but I still had to carry on for the people around me."

"Thank you, Ben," I replied sincerely. He somehow managed to make all this seem so simple when it was anything but.

"If you ever need to talk, you know where I'm at." He paused, and I heard someone shouting in the background. "I hate to do this, but I have to run. Please stay in touch."

"I will. I promise," I said.

"Goodbye," he said, and the phone clicked off.

I sat there in the silence of my apartment and tried my best to not think about the future. Ben was right, if I really did have a long life to live, why waste it thinking about tomorrow? I headed to Central Park, hoping that a long walk would clear my head.

Twenty

"I didn't know that you could cook," I teased Mark as I watched him working diligently in the kitchen to prepare us dinner. We were having steak, roasted vegetables, and a small filet of seared tuna—his take home prize from the fishing trip.

The guys had brought home a single bluefin tuna weighing in at one hundred pounds, which they shared amongst themselves. My mouth watered from the smells of the fish and the steak sizzling in the pan.

"I'm no Bobby Flay," he laughed, "but I can manage a steak and this pathetic, little piece of fish. I can't make any promises on the vegetables though."

"Hmph." I walked over to the oven with my glass of Argentinian wine, despite orders to stay out of the kitchen and relax. "So far so good."

I stood behind him and slipped my hands under his shirt, running them up and down his warm, muscled abdomen.

I wonder what my chances of burning dinner are if I have my way with her right now.

I hid my smile in the curve of his back. I didn't realize how much I'd missed him while he was gone. As he predicted, they had stayed out on the boat until Tuesday, and he'd called me as soon as he got home. I'd already made plans with Ashley but promised him I'd come over on Wednesday, both of us having to wait an extra day to see one another.

He seriously considered burning dinner when he finally resigned himself by saying, "You're going to make me burn it *all* if you keep doing that, Texas."

"I'm sorry." I went back to my spot at the island. "I'll leave you to it."

During dinner, he told me some of the highlights from his trip.

"On the first day, Nate thought he had a gigantic fish on the line and started getting cocky about it. It took him almost two hours to reel it in, only to find out that it was a five-foot-long shark."

"Holy crap!"

"Yeah! Then the idiot almost gets his fingers bitten off trying to get the hook out of its mouth with his bare hands instead of using the pliers. We tossed it back, of course."

"Idiot," I mumbled in between bites.

"Then Stephen—the one you met at the party—" he continued, "poor guy was seasick the entire time. One day he almost fell overboard barfing over the side of the boat."

"Aww," I said sincerely. I had liked Stephen. "Did he get to fish at all?"

"On the last day he felt well enough to do a little bit of fishing and caught a mackerel. It was too small to keep." He paused to take a sip of his wine. "We ended up playing cards most of the time though. It was a good time as usual."

"Sounds like fun!" I took a sip from my second glass of wine. "Who do I thank for catching this delicious tuna?"

"Well, Franky and George," he named them as if I knew who they were. "And a little bit of me. She wasn't huge by any means, but it still took the three of us over an hour to reel her in."

"Nice!" I took the last bite on my plate and reminisced about the last time I went fishing.

"What are you thinking about?" he asked.

"I was just thinking that I haven't been on a boat in years. We used to go all the time when I was younger," I responded. "Although, our trips were just day trips to a lake or down the river. Most of the time we'd park the boat on a sandbar and swim all day long."

I'd love to see you in a bikini, covered in sand.

I blushed, feeling the wine coursing through my veins.

He remained polite though and said, "That sounds nice."

I finished my glass of wine and said, "Dinner was amazing, thank you."

"You're welcome." He smiled. "More wine?"

"Why not?" I watched as he poured each of us our third glass of wine.

After clearing the table together, I asked, "Do you want to watch a movie or something?"

I was putting the last dish into the sink when he came and stood behind me, one of his hands making its way up my shirt, the other fumbling with the button on my jeans. He was so close that I could feel his chest rising and falling on my back as he breathed steadily.

He whispered in my ear, "Or something."

He turned me around quickly, not able to hold himself back any longer, and lifted me effortlessly onto the counter. His tongue tasted like sweet red wine as he kissed me fervently, determined to make up for the five days we missed. I wrapped my legs around his waist and dug my fingernails in his back, trying to pull him closer to me. He carried me to the couch, barely missing a beat in between kisses, where he took his time finishing what he'd started.

Later, we laid on the couch, still naked, watching *Rush Hour* for the third time together. It was the only movie that he owned on VHS—a gag gift from one of his friends last Christmas. Mark was lying on top of me, his head nestled on my bare chest.

I thought Mark had fallen asleep when I heard his thoughts loud and clear halfway through the movie.

I think I'm in love with this girl. It's still way too soon to tell her that, right? Damn this part is funny!

He was referring to the scene where Jackie Chan and Chris Tucker danced to "War" on their stakeout. He was laughing but I was still stuck on his thoughts of love.

Six months ago, I would have loved the idea of someone like Mark falling in love with me. Then again, six months ago I wouldn't have known that he was thinking about telling me he loved me. We would've been lying here in each other's silence, laughing at a silly movie. I also would have thought there was a possibility of having children and growing old with someone eventually.

Once again, I was at a crossroads with telling him about me in the hope that it would make this easier, or end it, thinking that it wasn't right to get close to someone knowing it couldn't last.

Why couldn't it last? I thought. Maybe I didn't have to marry him, or anyone else I dated. Having kids was never a priority for me, and since learning that I stopped aging on my thirtieth birthday, the entire idea of kids had disappeared. However, dating didn't have to be so complicated. It was okay to want companionship, even if temporary. I could date someone for several years before they noticed that I wasn't changing.

Still, I knew it wasn't fair to Mark because maybe he *was* thinking about those things. Although, I'd never heard him thinking of kids or marriage when we were together, that didn't mean he didn't want those things.

I decided at that moment that it was time for *the talk*. I knew I was falling for him too, but with all these other thoughts running through my mind, I'd pushed the feeling deep down. If I knew what his idea of the future looked like, maybe we could successfully be in a relationship for the time being, and I wouldn't have to feel bad about being with him now.

I thought, it's now or never.

"What are you thinking about?" I pried.

Random question, he thought, but answered casually with, "I'm wondering if Jackie Chan really did all of his own stunts."

Liar, I thought, knowing very well that he was still thinking about if it was too soon to tell me he loved me or not. "Can I ask you something?" I asked.

"Of course," he said while propping himself up on his arms to look me in the eyes.

"Where do you see this going?" I waited and then added, "*This* being us."

"I knew what you meant," he said slightly amused, then in a more serious tone, "I know that I enjoy being with you and I don't want that to end."

"But?"

And I think I love you.

"No but," he said avoiding his own thought. "Why are you asking?"

"No reason," I muttered.

Oh no, you're not getting off that easily. Girls don't just ask that for no reason. "You didn't ask that for no reason. Spit it out, Texas."

"I guess I just wanted to know if you saw this going somewhere or if we were just having fun?"

One of his eyebrows was raised in skepticism. *Liar.*

"If I'm being honest," I started, "I would have to say that I'm falling in love with you."

It was much easier saying it out loud knowing that he was thinking it too, especially since his face remained unchanged after I said it aloud.

"However," I continued, "I'm not in a place where I want a serious relationship."

What is she trying to say? At this he looked confused but still didn't say anything.

"What I'm trying to say is that I enjoy being with you too, and I also don't want it to end, but you should know that I have no interest in getting married and having kids—ever," I responded truthfully.

"If I may ask, why not?"

"It's complicated."

Complicated? What girl doesn't want marriage and kids? "Let me get this straight," he began slowly. "You're falling in love with me and want to keep seeing me, but not seriously because you don't ever want to get married or have kids?" *What? So you can see other people without the guilt of being tied down?*

I knew I had to say something to reassure him that what he was thinking was not what I wanted without him knowing that I'd heard him.

"Basically, yes, except that I'm not entirely against a serious relationship. I just don't want to waste your time if those are things that you want because I will never want the same thing." I ran my hands over his shoulders and through his hair, adding, "And I'm not saying all of this for permission to see other people either."

He maintained eye contact with me, trying to read my mind. *I guess that's every guy's dream, right? All the fun and no strings attached. Still seems strange.*

I remained quiet while he processed this information.

It's not like I'm going out ring shopping tomorrow. Hell, I hadn't even thought about that possibility since Crystal. Which I only considered marrying her because of her ultimatum to marry her or else she was leaving. I didn't even love her. Now, this amazing girl is telling me she loves me but will never want to take the next step.

I interrupted his thoughts and said, "I'm sorry to bring this up now. I understand if you need time to think about what you want."

"It does seem odd. Normally that's all girls want—you know, the big wedding and a pretty white dress," he said carefully, to which I screwed my face up in disgust at the idea. He smirked, relieved that he didn't offend me, and continued, "However, I appreciate you being upfront with me, and I think it's safe to say that I don't hear any wedding bells in my future... at least not in the near future."

"And you're okay with that?"

"For now, yes," he said matter-of-fact. *I'll stay on your hook as long as you want me to, Riley.*

"Plus," he said, turning his attention back to the movie, "there are plenty of women lined up ready to marry me when you're done with me."

"Oh please," I said, laughing. "You're so full of it."

He was laughing too, both of us happy to be done with this conversation. He faced me again and looked deep into my eyes before bending forward to softly touch his lips to mine. Mark kissed me slowly this time, not in any rush to get to the end. His movements were gentle but effective, sending chills all over my body every time his fingers brushed against my skin.

I vaguely heard the movie credits rolling on the television in the background when I whispered to Mark to take me to his bedroom.

It didn't take long and afterwards I nuzzled closer to Mark in bed, my heart still racing and his breathing coming rapidly. It was nearly the middle of the night, and my eyes were getting heavier as he lazily stroked my hair.

Right before he dozed off, I heard Mark mumble, "I love you, Riley Bandoni."

"I love you too, Mark Madison," I murmured back, not sure if he kept himself awake long enough to hear it.

***

I couldn't have been asleep for very long when I was woken up abruptly for the third time by the sound of wind rushing through the room and the golden-white glow surrounding an irritated looking woman.

She was small like Thomas—the person from the most recent vision—and dressed like she had stepped out of a fifties fashion magazine. She was wearing a white cotton shirt tucked into a flowing pink poodle skirt. Her blonde hair was perfectly curled, and her bright blue eyes popped next to her fair skin color.

Esther Willoughby is no longer with us.
Their ability has passed on to Louis Wilde.

After she had vanished, I noticed that I was sitting up in bed. I was breathless as a million thoughts were running through my mind.

"Is everything okay, Tex?" Mark asked sleepily, his hand resting on my arm.

"Yes," I said, urging myself to sound calm. "Just a bad dream."

He started snoring quietly again once he was assured that I was fine.

I wasn't fine though—two in one week. This wasn't good.

I got out of bed in search of something to drink or something to do. I desperately wanted to call Ben, but I couldn't. Even though he'd be awake after that vision too, I couldn't call another man from Mark's place, no matter the reason.

I knew for now that there was nothing to do but go back to sleep.

As I laid back down next to Mark, I had a feeling deep in my gut that everything was about to change.

Twenty-One

The next morning, I snuck out of bed early to shower and get ready for work before Mark woke up.

Once dressed, I stood there watching him sleep peacefully for a moment. After last night's vision, I didn't know what was going to happen next, but I figured it didn't include spending time with Mark anytime soon.

The thought made me sad, but it was clear that someone or something was after us.

I gently shook Mark to wake him and say goodbye.

"Why are you dressed?" he asked, still groggy.

"I have to stop at home before I head into work. I left some papers there that I need today."

It was a weak lie, but thankfully he bought it.

Bummer. "You can't stay for just a few minutes?" He pulled on my arm, tenderly trying to coax me back into bed with him.

"I wish I could," I said, kissing him on the cheek.

He groaned in resignation.

"Call me later, okay?" I smiled.

"I will," he said, grinning back and tucking a stray hair behind my ear. "Have a nice day."

When I arrived home, thankfully Ashley was in the bathroom, so I quickly found Ben's phone number and dialed.

It rang endlessly until finally his answering machine picked up. I glanced at the clock on my bedside table, which showed 7:18 a.m. Surely, he was awake even with him being an hour behind me.

I tucked the piece of paper with his number on it in my pocket, figuring that I would try again later at the office.

It was difficult to focus on work between thinking about my night with Mark and the third—technically fourth—vision. I wanted to know what Ben and the others were thinking. I periodically checked my voicemail back at the apartment for any calls from Ben, but there were none.

What's wrong with you? Ashley's voice at my door made me jump.

"Nothing, I just have a lot on my mind."

Apparently, I didn't sound convincing because she said, "In all the years that I've known you, I've never seen you look as distracted as you do now."

She came further into my office, closed the door behind her, and sat down. "Talk to me."

I considered telling her everything but decided to continue keeping this secret to myself for now, no matter how badly I wanted her advice on the subject.

I lied instead. "My dad is really sick. I'm not sure how sick because my mom is downplaying it, but they've admitted him to a hospital."

"Oh Riley, I'm so sorry," she said sincerely. "What happened?"

"His heart maybe?" I hated how easy it had become to lie. "I offered to go back home for a while to help my mom, but she told me not worry about it. Obviously, I'm worried though." The last part wasn't exactly a lie.

You should be! "Maybe you should just show up," she offered.

"That's what I was thinking but maybe I'm overthinking it, too." Again, not a lie.

"When did you find all this out?" she asked after a moment.

"She first called on Sunday, but I didn't think anything of it until I tried calling this morning to check in and there was no answer." I really wanted to talk to Ben.

"Maybe it was just too early," she said. "Why don't you try again?"

"Yeah, I will in a little bit." I smiled at the concerned look on her face.

"Are you going to be okay?"

"Yes, thanks Ash," I responded. "Like I said, I just have a lot on my mind."

Have you mentioned this to Mark?

"No, I didn't want to worry him with this." Having completely forgotten about Mark since Ashley walked in, my thoughts drifted back to him. We had basically declared our love for one another last night and here I was the next day, considering abandoning him for a group of people I barely knew.

"How are things between you and him?"

I couldn't stop the smile spreading across my face despite myself, and I told her about our conversation last night and saying 'I love you' to one another. It was nice to be truthful about one aspect of my life.

Her eyebrows were raised in astonishment. "You told him that *you* don't want to be in a committed relationship? Why would you do that?"

"Come on, with what I am, hearing his thoughts?" I said. "It can't last long. I'd have to tell him eventually and then what?" I lowered my voice and added, "Plus, whatever is going on with my dad, I may have to go home for a while, and I don't expect him to wait around for me."

"I guess so," she said. "But like you said, you don't even know what's going." *Are you sure that you're telling me everything?*

I looked up at Ashley's thought, her eyes intent on me.

Because you know you can tell me anything, right?

"I know," I answered. "I swear that's all."

She left without saying another word, and I called my answering machine once again.

To my relief there was one message from Ben.

"Hey Riley, it's me, Ben. I'm sure you're wondering about the vision from this morning—"

I heard the hesitation in his voice before he continued.

"—we all are. Odin, Elliot, and I are trying to reach out to the others to meet here in Logan for the time being. At least until we can figure out what's going on. Please call me so I know that you're okay."

I already felt on edge about everything going on, including the death dreams, and his message did nothing to mollify me. I deleted the message and called him back.

"Hello, this is Ben," his husky voice said after the first ring.

"Hey Ben, it's Riley. I just got your message—"

"Riley! Good! You're okay!" he shouted, cutting me off.

"Why wouldn't I be?" I asked, trying not to sound apprehensive. "Do you really think that we're all in some kind of danger?"

"We're not sure but something is definitely going on. The number of deaths in such a short period of time is uncommon for people like us."

"I figured."

"As I told you on Sunday, we've been trying to contact the others to make sure everyone is all right. Since then, everyone has decided to head to Logan, especially after this morning."

He waited for me to say something and when I didn't, he added, "Three of us are here already, including me. Tracey—the new one from a couple of months ago—and Lin—the one from the other day—are on their way with Odin and Elliot. Luckily, they were easy to track down. I'm glad you're all right because now all we need to do is track down this Louis person from this morning... and Amari."

"Who's Amari?"

"He's from India. Nice kid too. Before you, he was the youngest of us, but his change happened forty or fifty years ago. He typically stays in touch with Odin, but he's not been able to reach him, and no one locally has seen him in months."

"Could he be..." I didn't want to finish my train of thought seeing as how I didn't know Amari.

Ben caught on though and said reassuringly, "No, not Amari. I'm sure of that."

I heard voices in the background, as if a group of people had just entered the room.

"Hey there! Give me one minute..." Ben said, addressing the crowd. Then to me, he said, "Sorry, Elliot and Tracey just got here. How soon do you think you can be here?"

I knew before making this phone call that there was a potential that I'd have to go to Logan. Now, being asked when I could be there, I became indignant.

I didn't choose this life. I didn't want this life. Now I was expected to drop everything—a great job, an amazing friend, a wonderful boyfriend. And for what? A group of people who I barely knew and who didn't have the slightest clue as to what was happening to us.

If I left and this all turned out to be a big coincidence of deaths, I would risk losing my job, my boyfriend, and potentially my best friend when she finds out I'd been lying to her all this time.

"Riley?" Forgetting that I was on the phone, Ben's voice startled me back to reality.

"I'm sorry," I said, "this is all just too much."

"I understand how difficult it may seem to drop everything. We've all been there," he said. His voice remained calm as he continued. "If you need some time to think about it, that's fine. But please promise to check in with me daily so I know you're safe."

"Alright."

I felt like I owed him a better answer, as he'd been nothing but helpful to me. After all, my current predicament wasn't his fault.

"I've got to go, but I hope to see you soon. Goodbye, Riley."

"Goodbye, Ben."

I continued holding the receiver up to my ear, listening to the hum of the dial tone on the other end.

***

"Ashley, there's something that I need to tell you, but I need you to promise that you won't tell anyone else ever!" I expressed, unsmiling, "NO ONE! Not Alex, your dad, my parents, not even your diary!"

We were sitting face to face on the couch later that evening in our living room. After my phone call with Ben, I had decided that I was going to tell her everything, being that I desperately wanted her advice. I'd always known I could trust her with this information—after all, she was my best friend. I waited until we got home, knowing that I would have her full attention and there wasn't the possibility of anyone listening in on our conversation.

You're scaring me. Her face was blank and her eyes were round. "What's going on, Ry?"

"Promise me first!"

"I promise!"

"You were right earlier when you thought there was something that I wasn't telling you," I began. "First off, my dad isn't sick."

I'm listening.

"Please know that the reason I hadn't told you any of this before was because I was still trying to comprehend it all myself as well."

"Okay," she responded slowly.

I took a deep breath and told her everything from the beginning; how when I went back to Logan, Ben told me the truth of who I was now, how there were others—but I didn't give away any of their names—and how I stopped aging the night that I started hearing thoughts. I also mentioned the visions and how they signified that one of us had died and our ability transferred to another person.

She remained quiet as I spoke, taking in what I was telling her, her face unchanged.

I waited for her to say or think something after I ended with the conversation between Ben and me earlier that morning. When she didn't say anything, I added, "Again, I'm sorry that I didn't tell you sooner, but like I said, I've been trying to process it all myself. Plus..."

"It wasn't only your secret to tell," she said, finishing my thought.

I felt relieved that she understood where I was coming from and that she wasn't upset with me.

"Exactly. And now this... I don't know what to do!" I shouted a little too loudly. "A part of me wants to pack up and go, but then again, I've got my life here—you, work, and..."

"And Mark?" she asked, again finishing my thought for me.

"Yes, and Mark."

Neither one of us said anything for a few moments. Ashley was thinking to herself, but I was barely listening to what she was saying.

"For what it's worth," she said after a few minutes, "I think you should go."

"You do?" I replied in shock.

"If these people are like you, and you're all in some kind of trouble, you should probably be with them, right?"

I didn't know what to say, so she added, "You can always come back here, Riley, it's New York City for crying out loud. People come and go all the time, and it'll always be here. You can find a new job. As wonderful as he might be, if Mark isn't here when you come back, there are a million other guys out there. Also, from what you're telling me, it sounds like you have all the time in the world to meet someone else. As for me," she continued, "I'll always be here for you no matter what. But whatever is going on with you and these people seems more important than all those other things."

Tears welled up in my eyes and I leaned forward to hug her. "Thank you. I honestly don't know what I'd do without you."

Twenty-Two

"I'm still unsure of what to do," I said, releasing Ashley from my embrace, "Also, if I do decide to go, when should I go? Just pack up and leave tomorrow? Next week?"

"Why don't you come to Houston with me for a couple of days?" Ashley offered. "It'll give you a few days to get away and think about what you want to do, and I'll have someone to hang out with while Alex is working."

I had forgotten that she was leaving in the morning to go stay with Alex down in Houston for the weekend. He called her the other day to tell her that he was going to be stuck working down there for a couple of weeks and that he'd booked her a flight for this weekend.

"He mentioned that I could bring a friend if I wanted, so I don't think it will be an issue."

I never told Ashley how uncomfortable he made me at Mark's birthday party, and I was still skeptical of being anywhere near him. She did say he would be working most of the weekend, and I wouldn't mind getting away for a few days to think through all of this. If I did decide to go to Logan, I could always rent a car in Houston and drive from there.

"Are you sure he wouldn't mind?"

"Not at all!" She jumped up to grab the phone. "I'll call him now! And you don't have to worry about anything! He already told me he'd pay for the flight if you or someone tagged along."

"That's awfully nice of him," I said, half smiling. "When do we leave?"

"First thing in the morning!"

Before she could dial Alex's number, the phone started ringing.

What if it's Mark? Ashley thought.

My heart sank into the pit of my stomach. I wasn't ready to talk to him just yet.

"If it is, tell him I'm in the shower or something. I'll call him back later."

Ashley answered as I went into my room to pack. I heard her saying, "Hey Mark. She's in the shower but I'll tell her to call you when she gets—"

I shut the door to my room and started packing, not knowing what to pack when I didn't know how long I'd begone.

It took some time, but I filled up a duffle bag with clothes and grabbed a few valuable items that I couldn't bring myself to part with for the time being.

After showering, I met Ashley back in the living room and asked, "What did he say?"

"Nothing really," she said without looking up from the magazine she was reading, referring to the call with Mark. "He was just checking in and said it was fine to call him back later. What are you going to say to him?"

"I meant what did Alex say?" I responded. "And I have no clue. I guess I'll just keep spinning this web of lies that I'm in."

Just tell him you're going home for the weekend because your dad is sick... That's what you told me, wasn't it?

I snorted, noting the hint of sarcasm. "I said I was sorry."

"I'm only joking, except for the part about using the same excuse on Mark," said Ashley. "Also, Alex said it was cool."

"See you in the morning, then." I took the phone with me back into my room.

I called Ben first, thinking it would be the easiest of the two phone calls, to let him know about my temporary change in plans to go to Alex's house in Houston first.

"Are you sure you can trust this person?" He sounded concerned, which I didn't blame him for considering everything that was going on.

"I have no reason not to trust him," I lied. "Ashley trusts him, and I trust Ashley." I added when he didn't say anything, "I'll call you when I get there."

He was satisfied enough for now with that response. Before we hung up, he informed me that Odin and Lin had made it into town earlier in the evening.

I sat on the bed and stared absently at the phone in my hand. I dreaded having to call Mark, knowing that I was only calling to lie to him.

"Hi there," I said cheerfully when he answered.

"Hello gorgeous," his soft, sweet voice said from the other end of the line. "How was your day?"

"Busy as usual. How about yours?"

"Lonely after you left, but I managed." I pictured the dimple on his cheek, and that playful look in his eyes when he was being flirtatious.

I felt sad thinking that I may not get to see that again for a while—or ever again.

"You're a big boy," I teased, "I'm sure you were just fine without me."

"Seriously! The bed was so cold, and I had nothing to snuggle but my pillow."

"You poor thing." I giggled as he started laughing at himself. "Didn't you tell me that you had a big meeting to go to today?"

"Yes, it was a lunch meeting with my father and one of his partners."

I listened as he divulged the details of his lunch, which he deemed to be boring and mundane. However, his father's partner was an investor from California.

"He said he may know a guy who I might be interested in talking to about a few investment opportunities." He paused and then said, "We're going to have dinner tomorrow night."

I remember Mark telling me once about how he liked the idea of investing in the little guys—people who had inventions or ideas of inventions but no resources to help get them started. Although he was never sure how to break out in that field and away from his father.

"That's great!" I said sincerely.

"Yeah, we'll see. I'm curious to see what he has to say."

"For sure! It's still a wonderful opportunity either way."

"Thanks, Texas. Any plans for this evening?" he asked. "Want to come over again?"

"No," I said and quickly recovered with, "No to any plans this evening. As for coming over, I'd love to, but I can't."

"Everything okay?"

"Yes—I mean no." I knew fumbling my words was going to make the lie sound even more unbelievable. "I got a call from my mom today. My dad's not doing well, so I'm flying out early in the morning to go home for the weekend."

"Why did you let me go on about that stupid lunch!?" he shouted. Then he lowered his voice and said, "I'm sorry to hear that."

I laughed a little. "It's fine. Really. Just a last-minute trip is all."

"I get it. Please let me know if there's anything that I can do."

"I really appreciate that, and I will."

I hated this. Mark was too sweet of a guy. I began to think that it was better to leave and never return for his sake. He deserved better than the labyrinth of deception that I was giving him.

I also thought that if I ever did return, he deserved the truth, and if he still wanted to be with me after that, then at least I wouldn't have to feel guilty about lying to him anymore.

Now was not the time to tell him though.

"I do have one thing," I started.

"What's that?"

"Don't blow it at your dinner tomorrow."

He laughed aloud. "I'm not worried about that dinner whatsoever. I mean, it'd be nice to have someone bite on the ideas that I have but it's no big deal if nothing comes of it."

"Mhmm," I hummed. "Go big or go home, right?"

"Right."

I was ready to go to bed but not ready to say goodbye to him yet. We didn't speak for a few minutes, happily enjoying each other's silence. I thought of this morning, which seemed so long ago now, his warm body wrapped around mine.

Finally, I said, "Well, I've got an early flight, so I should probably get going. I'll call you on Saturday and you can tell me all about your dinner, okay?"

"It's a date," he said. "Have a good flight."

***

The following day we arrived in Houston shortly after lunch. Luckily, we were both able to dodge baggage claim and headed straight to the exit. There, we saw a tall bald man waiting for us and holding a sign with Ashley's name on it.

"Hi," Ashley approached the man. "I'm Ashley Hannigan."

"Hello, Ms. Hannigan. Welcome to Houston," the man said, barely smiling. "My name is Taylor. Let me grab your bags for you."

He opened the car door for us, reaching for our bags as we slid into the back seat of the town car, and closed the door behind us.

"Fancy," I muttered to Ashley as he was putting the bags into the trunk.

The corner of her mouth twitched into a smile as Taylor was buckling himself into the driver's seat.

Taylor seemed nice enough, though he looked as if he hadn't slept in days. There were dark circles under his eyes and deep lines crinkled on either side of them. When he did speak, his voice sounded raspy, like he'd been yelling at someone. He kept his sentences short, and his thoughts seemed scripted. I thought that his rough looking appearance made him look much older than what his age might have actually been, but it was hard to tell.

I remembered the last time that I visited Houston when my sister and I were teenagers. Our dad came here for a business trip, and he brought us along since we weren't in school at the time. Even though we spent most of our time walking around downtown and shopping at the stores near our hotel, I thought that the area surrounding the airport looked unchanged. The air outside was the same take-your-breath-away, hot, humid air, much like it was during the summers back home.

Traffic slowed to a standstill, and I hoped we wouldn't be stuck in it for long. We'd been up longer than the sun; I was hungry and ready to get this airport stench off me.

Fortunately, we exited the interstate within minutes, and I gazed out the window in awe as we passed several massive houses surrounding a lake. The car slowed down in front of an elegant two-story home with a half-circle driveway in the front yard, which Taylor pulled into slowly. It was one of the bigger homes that I had seen on the drive in, with four large white columns spanning across the front of the house. Like all the other houses, the lawn was immaculate and the gardens lush and well-kept.

Whoa.

I heard Ashley's thought mimicking mine.

Taylor led us, with our bags in his hands, to the ornate front door. Before he could open the door, a small, rotund woman beat him to it, greeting us from the other side.

"Welcome," she said through a forced grin. "Please, come in."

Like Taylor, she looked as if she hadn't slept in days. Her small, beady eyes also had circles underneath them and crow's feet on either side. Her hair was untidy and had several gray streaks showing through the pale brown. She seemed anxious and gave me the feeling that she had more important things to be doing other than being here to greet us.

"My name is Norma," she said listlessly as she ushered us through the foyer and into the living room.

Both areas of the home were decorated entirely in white, barring three large abstract paintings hanging on the walls. There was a large sectional sofa placed stylishly in the center of the room but looked as if it had never been used. To my right was a massive fireplace, surrounded by brick framework which was painted stark white to match the walls. On my left was a staircase leading to the second floor, and compared to the rest of the home, an undersized kitchen, which also looked as if it had never been touched.

I thought that it felt more like being in a museum rather than someone's home as it was void of any evidence that someone lived here. I took into consideration that Alex was a bachelor who had recently moved to New York, but even Mark's apartment had little pieces of him placed here and there; family photos, trinkets from traveling, a fruit bowl on the counter, et cetera.

Norma spoke after halting in the living room. "Please let me know if there is anything you need during your stay."

Which hopefully, will be nothing, I heard her mutter to herself. Her eyes widened after she noticed me scowling at her.

"Thank you so much, Norma," Ashley said oblivious to her rudeness.

"Yes," I said graciously. "Thank you."

Norma looked away, embarrassed, and I wasn't sure if she thought that she'd said it aloud or if she recognized how rude she was being to her boss's guests.

"Mr. Matthews wanted me to inform you that he will not be joining you until later this evening as he's been held up at work," she uttered to Ashley, avoiding eye contact with me. "Please make yourselves at home though, and I'll be happy to show you to your rooms when you're ready."

"That would be great! We'd like to freshen up a little, right Riley?" Ashley said.

"Yes, please," I answered.

What's wrong with you? Can you believe this place?

I smiled briefly at Ashley to acknowledge her thought.

Norma said to Ashley, "Your room is upstairs. If you will follow me, please."

This time she faced me and said more politely, "I'll be right back to show you to your room, Ms. Bandoni."

Ashley shouted to me as they disappeared up the stairs, *Meet me back down here in an hour!*

Twenty-Three

While I waited for Norma to return, I continued to admire Alex's home and noticed for the first time a small rectangular pool through a pair of glass French doors. The sunlight's rays were bouncing off the pool and dancing on the bare walls behind me.

However, the selling point of his home was not its vast size or the sparkling pool in the backyard, but the stunning view of the lake beyond the pool. It was a huge lake, but I could still make out the small outlines of similarly massive homes sitting along the opposite side of the bank. I noticed long stretches of wooded areas running along the lake as well, and I wondered idly if they were left undeveloped on purpose or if they were waiting for someone to come in and build something.

I saw several people flying across the glassy water in their boats, and a few that were parked to fish along the tree line. I had become hypnotized watching the water move away from the nearest boat when I heard Norma's heavy steps coming down the stairs behind me.

"This way please, Ms. Bandoni," she said curtly as she headed toward a hallway on the side of the fireplace without looking back to see if I was following her.

The hallway had several doors within it, all of which were closed. Mine was the last room on the left. She opened the door, and I saw that my bag had already been placed on a bench at the end of the bed. She quickly showed me around the adjoining bathroom and left without saying another word.

I locked the door after she left and admired the bedroom that I was given, which was large enough to be the master suite. There was a king-size bed which had at least ten pillows placed decoratively on top of a fluffy white duvet. I was pleased to see that I had a magnificent view of both the pool and the lake outside the windows.

I started to relax a little, thinking that this was a perfect place to get away and think about what I was going to do next.

The phone sitting on the bedside table reminded me that I had promised to call Ben once I got settled in Houston. I sat on the edge of the bed and dialed the phone number that I had memorized by now.

It was a quick phone call where he informed me that Elliot thought he may have found Louis—however, if it was the right Louis, he lived in England. He and Elliot were going to fly out to England tomorrow morning while Odin stayed in Logan with the others.

After hanging up with him, I took a long, hot shower. Feeling rejuvenated, I made my way back into the living room to find Ashley. Halfway down the hallway I stopped briefly, noticing a different colored knob on one of the doors across from my room. It only caught my eye because everything else in the home had been colored white or black, while this doorknob was a bronze and faded from heavy use.

I wasn't sure why I felt the need to try, but out of curiosity, I attempted to open it, knowing very well that it would be locked. I wasn't surprised when the handle didn't turn, and I figured it was just an old storage closet.

I found Ashley sitting on a lounge chair out by the pool, reading a magazine.

"There you are!" she said over the top of the magazine. "Can you believe this place? It's amazing! And the master bedroom is huge! There are three closets... three!"

I listened as she described Alex's bedroom upstairs and the latest celebrity gossip that she was reading about while I thought about Mark, Ben, and the mysterious door in the hallway.

"Riley!? Did you hear me? What do you think?" Ashley shouted, snapping me out of my thoughts.

"I'm sorry; I zoned out," I said apologetically. "What did you say?"

"I said," she repeated, "Alex won't be able to join us for dinner, but he recommended a few places downtown. Are you good with that?"

"Yeah, that sounds great." I smiled.

I thought it was odd that he paid for our flights, was too busy with work to greet us when we arrived, and now he wouldn't be able to have dinner with us.

"Was Alex here?" I asked.

"Just for a few minutes to tell me hello," she said. "Why?"

I voiced my concerns, but she simply responded with, "He's just really busy with work I guess," before refocusing her attention on her magazine.

"Tell me again what he does for work?"

"Something to do with medical research, I think."

"Where is he from?" I prodded.

She put her magazine down. "What's with all the questions?"

"I'm just curious," I said. "I don't know much about the person whose house I'm staying at."

"He's never said, but I know that he's lived in different places all over the world because of his job."

I decided not to ask any more questions since Ashley seemed unfazed by his behavior. Instead, I turned and stared out at the water.

✳✳✳

After an evening of lying out by the pool, Taylor drove Ashley and me to a place in town called Blue Man Two—one of Alex's recommendations of places to go—which turned out to be a pretentious cocktail bar with only three other people sitting in the lounge.

Maybe just stay for one drink?

I rolled my eyes and laughed. "Sure."

We sat at the furthest end of the bar, where we were instantly greeted by a bartender who looked bored out of his mind.

"Hello ladies. What can I get for you this evening?" He was slender and his greasy, jet-black hair was slicked back.

Ashley asked eagerly, "Do you have any food? We're starving!"

I didn't realize how hungry I was until she said it. Neither of us had eaten all day.

"Sorry, no," he replied ruefully. *I keep telling Don that he needs to put some appetizers on the menu. It'll make more people actually want to come to this crappy joint.*

I heard Ashley thinking simultaneously, *Want to go?*

They both looked to me for a decision to be made when I said, "Whiskey on the rocks, please." I raised my eyebrows at Ashley, insisting that she order.

"Manhattan for me."

"Coming right up," he said and left to make our drinks.

"He was thinking how no one ever comes in and stays because there's no food, so I felt bad," I explained as she looked questioningly at me. "One drink won't hurt, plus we're not driving."

She didn't answer so I added, "It's kind of a cool place."

We both looked around and saw that the bar was in fact really dull. The bar spanned the entire length of the building and consisted of every liquor that you could imagine but was otherwise unimpressive. The walls were painted dark green but had pink and red lights shining on the wall from above. Instead of tables and chairs, there were black lounge chairs and beige couches scattered around randomly.

They were playing what sounded like elevator music, making me think that we might fall asleep if we stayed here too long.

Ashley laughed at me, knowing that the look on my face gave away that we were thinking the same thing about this place.

The bartender returned with our drinks and said, "I'm Russell by the way. Let me know if you need anything."

"Thank you," I responded.

At least the drinks are good, Ashley thought as she took a sip of her Manhattan.

"See, it's all good." I smiled. "Cheers!"

This time she rolled her eyes at me. "Well," she started. *Have you decided what you're going to do?*

"Can we talk about anything but that tonight?"

She understood and let it go immediately, changing the subject to work.

We stayed at Blue Man Two for another hour, having struck up a conversation with Russell. He and Ashley had a friendly argument over who was the better rock band, Red Hot Chili Peppers or Incubus, after Ashley suggested that he turn off the elevator music.

I tried to point out that while they were both rock bands, their styles of music were completely different, so it was a moot point of who was the better band. Neither of them wanted to agree aloud, and I laughed as they picked two other bands to argue about.

After our second drink, we couldn't stave off our hunger any longer. Russell recommended a bar a few doors down called The Iron Handle.

"They have a couple of pool tables and a decent menu," he said as we paid our tab.

"Thanks, Russell," Ashley and I said in unison.

We walked down the street and found the place easily—it being the liveliest place on the block. The music was loud, but at least it wasn't elevator music, and the thick, smoky air hit you like a brick wall upon entering the door. We went to the bar and ordered two beers and nachos.

While we waited for our food, we found an empty spot by the pool tables and watched other people play. The place reminded me of when I was in college. My friends and I would go out on Friday night to the local bar and have mini pool tournaments. I hadn't played since then, and while it was always just for fun, my friends and I became surprisingly good at playing.

"Have you ever played?" I asked Ashley.

"Once," she said, watching four guys battle over the eight ball with a wad of hundreds laying on the table. "A long time ago."

"Let's try and play once the crowd dies down," I suggested. "That way we don't end up playing someone for money."

She laughed. "Good idea."

Instead of the crowd thinning out, more people crammed into the building as the night wore on. We were having a great time though; our hunger had vanquished for the time being thanks to the nachos, and the beers were going down easy. Several guys approached us, offering to buy Ashley and me a drink, to which Ashley politely declined, saying her boyfriend would be here any minute.

I was surprised that the normally flirtatious Ashley was being so reserved.

We started talking with two girls, Jane and Maggie, whose boyfriends hadn't stopped playing pool since they arrived. They were much younger than us, but I wouldn't have known by the way they acted compared to the other groups of girls in the bar, except that they told us they were all still in college. Jane and Maggie were from the Houston area, and their boyfriends—Cameron and Jonathan—were from Louisiana.

Finally, a little after midnight, Jonathan and Cameron gave up on their pool game and let us have their table to play doubles with Jane and Maggie.

It took Ashley two games to get the hang of it, but she wasn't half bad after that. We all lost track of the time while playing and had been laughing so much that the muscles in my cheeks ached. I noticed that our game had drawn a sizeable crowd of spectators, half of them cheering on Ashley and me, and the other half cheering for Jane and Maggie. After the sixth game, and God knows how many drinks, Ashley and I left our new friends in search of Taylor to bring us home.

We found him parked outside the bar, asleep in the driver's seat. Ashley stumbled toward the car and knocked softly on the window, jolting him from his slumber.

"Hi," she said innocently.

"Ready to go?" Taylor said groggily.

"Yes, please," Ashley said as she climbed into the backseat.

The ride back to Alex's place was quiet. Ashley fell asleep on my shoulder, and I stayed awake—partially to keep an eye on the sleepy Taylor.

I wondered how Mark's dinner had gone this evening and considered calling him when we got back to the house. I changed my mind when I saw on the dashboard of the car that it was almost four o'clock in the morning.

I made a mental note to myself that if I decided to stay in New York, I would have to find a pool bar to go to with Mark to see if he was any good. However, the thought of playing pool with Mark reminded me that if I chose to go to Logan with Ben, there was a chance that I may never see Mark again.

Twenty-Four

Thanks to my overzealous mixture of whiskey, beer, and vodka shots, I woke up the next morning with a horrible headache. I rolled reluctantly out of bed and took a long hot shower in hopes that removing the stench of cigarette smoke and stale beer would make my hangover go away.

Much to my disappointment, it didn't.

While I was getting dressed, I stared out the window at the lake and thought that a walk around the neighborhood and some fresh air might help. It would also give me some time alone to think about the one thing I'd been avoiding thinking about since I arrived.

I stopped in the kitchen to see if Ashley was awake but found no sign of her or anyone else. However, there was a fresh pot of coffee and a tray of fruit laid out on the counter.

I poured myself a cup of coffee and grabbed a banana before sneaking out the front door.

The sidewalk ran in front of several of the neighboring homes before cutting down the property line in between two massive homes. It led to a path along the lake, through one of the wooded areas that I had noticed yesterday. Much like the lake back in Logan, it had places for people to picnic or sit on benches facing the water.

I walked over a mile before sitting on a bench, thankful that my headache was gone now. From where I was sitting, I could barely make out the back of Alex's home.

There were a lot of other people out as well, attracted, like me, by the warm sun beating down and a cool breeze blowing in from the lake. I watched as people jogged or biked past me and families strolled along the lake with their children.

For a while, I sat there, sipping my coffee and listening to all the noises around me; kids shouting playfully, the water lapping on the shore, and birds chirping in the trees. It was peaceful, and for a brief moment, I forgot why I was here. I forgot about Mark and Ben. I forgot that I was here to decide where I was going next.

Were things always going to be this complicated in this new life of mine? Would I always be running from something or someone?

Ben never mentioned anything like living on the run the night that he revealed everything to me.

It was a nice thought in theory—to be able to start over whenever I wanted and wherever I wanted. However, I also liked the idea of finding someone to spend the rest of my life with in one place.

I wondered how much of the latter idea was due to Mark. I couldn't remember the last time that I even remotely thought of settling down with anyone before him. I had dated but always stayed focused on my career and getting out of Texas and into a big city. I'd accomplished that and didn't have enough time to think about the rest before my life-altering birthday.

Now, barely six months after my change, I was having to make a choice between one life over the other.

Or did I?

I knew going to Logan to be with the others and figure out who—or what—was after us was the right thing to do, even if I still wasn't sure how I would be helpful.

Not to mention, Ashley had a point in saying that New York would always be there. I could easily find another job, no matter how much I loved mine. Plus, if Mark wasn't there when I came back, someone else would be. All in all, I could go to Logan and potentially pick up where I left off whenever I returned. If not, I thought I'd be content with the possibility of having to start over.

If what Ben told me was true about being *semi*-immortal—I still had my doubts—then I had time to shape my life the way I wanted.

I was satisfied with the conclusion I'd come up with, and I was beginning to formulate 'what if' scenarios when a flash of bright red hair caught my eye in the direction of Alex's house. I knew it was Ashley wandering around the pool, most likely in search of me, so I made my way back to the house.

There you are! I heard Ashley shout as I came through the front door.

"Good morning!" I said, feeling better than I did when I left.

"Good morning!" she responded cheerily. "Where have you been?"

"I went for a walk around the neighborhood. It's very pretty around here."

"Yeah, it is."

"What time did you get up?"

"Not long ago." She blushed. "Alex woke up when I got in last night and... well..." *We stayed up for a while after that.*

"I see," I replied. "And where is he now?"

"He ran out earlier this morning, but he said he'd be back around lunch." She took a sip from the mug in her hand before finishing. "He said that he wanted to take both of us out for dinner around four though, if that's okay with you."

"Whatever you want," I said smiling. "I'm just along for the ride."

"Good deal," she responded and then asked very vaguely, "Did you have some time to think things over?"

"I think so, I—" I was cut off by the sudden appearance of Norma to announce that brunch was ready on the back patio.

"I'll tell you later," I added as we made our way outside.

***

Ashley advised that Alex was taking us somewhere fancy for dinner, so I dressed myself in a shimmering tank top and black pants with short heels. It was half past three when I met Ashley in the kitchen, who was wearing a short, tight black dress with heels tall enough to match my height. In front of her was an open bottle of champagne for us to drink while we waited for Alex to pick us up.

He had never made it back here at lunch like he promised, but we didn't mind as we laid out by the pool all afternoon until it was time to start getting ready.

She was getting ready to pour us a second glass when Taylor walked in and said, "Good evening, ladies. I will be driving you to Le Rouge where Mr. Matthews will be joining you."

Of course, I thought to myself.

Ashley looked disappointed and put the bottle down on the counter.

She caught me looking at her and thought to herself, *It's fine. He probably got tied up or something.*

Le Rouge was a short drive from Alex's neighborhood. The building was set in the parking lot of a high-end strip mall. The outside was iron colored and had fire-lit lanterns all along the front wall. Taylor drove us to the front door, where a valet was waiting to open our door for us.

When we entered, the maître d' greeted us politely. "Good evening, what name is your reservation under?"

"Alex Matthews," Ashley said confidently.

"Oh yes. Right this way, Ms. Hannigan." He gestured us to follow him. "Mr. Matthews is already here."

The restaurant was smaller on the inside than I imagined it would be, especially considering the enormous size of the building from the outside. There couldn't have been more than twenty or thirty tables inside and all were decorated with white tablecloths and plates. Silver utensils—one for each course—were lined out neatly on white linen napkins.

Alex was sitting at a table large enough for ten people in the center of the room, deeply engrossed in the wine list.

"Hi baby!" Ashley said excitedly, announcing our arrival before the host could.

Alex set the menu on the table, beamed a charming smile at her, and stood to greet us.

I had a sinking feeling in the pit of my stomach, remembering the feelings that I had the last time I encountered him and hoped I wouldn't feel it again.

Alex embraced Ashley and kissed her softly on the cheek. "Hello darling." He released her and pulled her chair out for her as the scrawny host pulled my chair out on the other side of the table.

He sat back down next to Ashley and said to me, "Nice to finally see you in a more proper setting, Ms. Bandoni."

"Please, call me Riley," I said, placing my napkin in my lap. "But yes, it is. Especially after all you've done for us this weekend. Thank you."

"It's really no problem," he said coolly. "I hope you are both enjoying your time in Houston."

I could tell why Ashley was so infatuated with him. Besides being remarkably handsome, he seemed like a true gentleman. He spoke in a way that was calm and calculated, making you hang on every word he said.

We were halfway through dinner before I realized that I was experiencing those same strange whirls of emotion like the night of Mark's birthday, except somehow it felt different this time. Unlike that night, where I felt angry and jealous, this time I felt a strong sense of admiration, like I'd do anything he asked of me. This time though, I felt more in control of myself.

I took a long sip from my glass of wine and tried to focus my attention on something else—like the thoughts of the couple behind me. The guy behind me was planning to propose to his girlfriend during dessert and was trying to keep his cool throughout dinner so that he didn't ruin his own surprise. Unfortunately for him, his girlfriend already knew what he was planning and was growing impatient with every moment that he didn't do it.

Luckily, Ashley was doing most of the talking right now, so Alex and I sat there and listened, responding only when necessary.

I was hyperaware of Alex's stares in my direction when Ashley wasn't looking, and for the first time, I realized that I hadn't heard a thought from him all night. I knew that it wasn't uncommon to cross paths with visual thinkers. However, it made him that much more intriguing.

Lost in my thoughts, I didn't realize that both Ashley and Alex were staring at me now.

"Ry, Alex was asking where you went to undergrad," she repeated his question.

"Oh, sorry," I answered. "I went to Texas A&M for undergrad."

"That's a great school, and not far from here," Alex responded.

"No, not far at all," I acknowledged politely.

"Are you from around here then?" he asked.

"Kind of," I began. "I mean I'm from Texas, but not this part."

He waited for me to offer more information, but as I took a gulp of water, I decided it was time to turn the conversation onto him.

"What about you?" I inquired. "Are you from around here?"

"Not quite," he said.

Realizing that wasn't enough of an answer, he added, "I'm not really from anywhere. I've moved around a lot."

"How did you end up in Houston?"

What's with the interrogation?

I ignored Ashley's thought and waited for Alex to answer.

"Early in my career, I predicted that my business would thrive best in the growing economy that Houston has to offer," he explained arrogantly. "And I was right in doing so."

"What is it that you do exactly?"

"A little of this and a little of that," he said, a sly grin forming slightly on his face. He finished his glass of wine and turned to Ashley, clearly done with my questioning, "Do you want dessert, darling?"

"You know I do," she muttered as she ran her fingers up and down his arm, hinting that she meant him and not the sugary options on the menu.

Once we were back at the house, Ashley convinced me to stay up a little while longer for a nightcap.

"Just one," I told her. "I'm still exhausted from last night. Plus, I think I'm going to head out early in the morning to go home for a couple of days."

Oh really?! So, you decided to go to Logan?

I flashed a quick smile at Ashley, answering her thought.

"I can pay you back for the flight if you need me to, Alex," I offered.

"There's no need. The trip was my treat," he said. "I can probably trade the flight in for a rental car if you'd like?"

"That's very kind of you, but I'll be alright. Thank you anyway," I said, adding, "Thank you again for having me. It's been a nice little getaway."

"I apologize that I've been so busy with work this weekend," he admitted. "I wish I had more time to show you both around the city."

"It's no problem at all, babe," Ashley said. "Like Riley said, it's been a nice getaway just hanging around here."

"I've been to Houston plenty of times anyway," I said. "Ash, maybe you can stay a little longer, that way Alex can show you around without a third wheel here."

Way to put him on the spot! Then she added aloud, "I'd love to, but only if you don't mind me hanging around?"

"That would be wonderful," Alex replied, Ashley not noticing the slight change in his tone of voice. "Let me go grab another bottle of wine."

"Isn't he amazing?" Ashley whispered when he was out of earshot.

"He's something," I said, smiling to hide my true feelings, which were still vague.

She grabbed my hand and said, "Good luck tomorrow."

It felt like she was saying goodbye to me forever.

"Thank you... for everything," I said. "Don't worry. I'll be back in New York as soon as possible."

Alex's strange behavior was the least of my worries now. Ashley liked him and that was enough for me.

Alex came back with a new bottle of wine and filled all three of our glasses. We raised them in a toast—one to the weekend, one to the future, and one for safe travels home. I took a sip, savoring the smooth and fruity taste of the scarlet liquid.

Out of the corner of my eye, I noticed Alex watching me intently over the rim of his glass. It was the last thing I saw before everything went black.

Twenty-Five

The nightmare of being trapped inside a dark box with no way out was slowly fading away as I began to regain consciousness. My entire body felt too heavy to move, and I wondered how long I'd been asleep. I could tell there was a bright light shining from somewhere above me, but my eyes were swollen shut, and I didn't attempt to open them yet.

A sharp, stabbing pain throbbed consistently in the middle of my forehead, and my mouth was bone dry. I felt far worse than the hangover I'd had earlier—or yesterday maybe—and for a second all I could think about was drinking a large glass of water.

As I regained my senses, I blindly took in my surroundings. I knew I wasn't lying on the king-sized guest bed, nor was I on the poolside lounge chair, the last place that I recalled being. The mattress, which was smaller than a twin bed, was covered in thin, rough cotton sheets. Like a hospital, it smelled of strong cleaning supplies, making me think that Ashley and Alex had to take me to an emergency room for alcohol poisoning or something else that I couldn't remember.

It was too quiet for a hospital though. Actually, the only noise I could hear was the buzzing of the overhead lighting.

Curiosity persuaded me to try and open my eyes, but deep down I had a feeling that I already knew what was happening.

My first try was unsuccessful after being blinded by a blazing flash of white from the fluorescent lights on the ceiling, sharpening the pain in my head. I took a deep breath, turned my head slowly to one side, and tried again. This time I found myself staring at a solid white wall only a couple of inches away from my face.

It took a few minutes to steady my vision, but I was finally able to move my head around where I saw two more similar white walls and one wall constructed entirely of glass. The back wall contained the outline of a doorway in it, which I presumed was a small bathroom, considering all that was in this room was the bed that I was still lying on and a small table which matched the furniture in Alex's home.

I felt my heart pounding in my ears but took several deep breaths, the words 'stay calm' scrolling across my mind like a news ticker. Panicking wasn't going to do me any good at this point.

I took my time sitting up, realizing that I was still wearing the same clothes I wore for dinner with Alex and Ashley. I also noticed that my duffle bag was placed on the floor next to my bed. A wave of nausea came over me, and I closed my eyes, briefly trying to keep it down.

Once I was in control of my nerves, I glanced around the room again. The three solid walls looked like they were made of concrete and then painted chalk white. There was a door set within the glass wall which I saw could only be opened and locked from the outside. On the same wall was one of those boxes that doctors used to pass medicine through for patients in clean rooms. An empty room sat directly across from the one I was in, whose design mirrored mine, and between both rooms ran a narrow hallway. From where I was sitting, I couldn't see down either end of it.

I closed my eyes, this time taking it all in. I was confident that I knew where I was and who was behind it, but now all I wanted to know was why he was doing this.

"You're much calmer than the others were."

I stiffened at the sound of his honeyed voice.

I looked up and glared at Alex, whose dark eyes were staring back at me from the other side of the glass, a superior grin plastered on his face.

Considering the circumstances, I *was* extraordinarily calm, despite the lump in my throat and the steady thrum of my heart beating in my chest. The adrenaline coursing through my veins kept me from faltering, even when I saw that he was holding a glass of water in one hand.

He noticed my quick glance toward the glass and snickered. Alex stepped forward and placed the water in the pass-through box along with two pills.

"Take these and drink this," he commanded.

I looked suspiciously from him to the glass of water.

"If I wanted you dead, you'd be dead," he said as he casually placed his hands in his pockets.

I didn't want to do anything that he asked of me, thinking it might be a sign of weakness on my part, but I could feel my throat burning from dehydration.

Plus, he was right; he could've easily killed me already.

No, I thought, he needs me. I just wasn't sure what for yet.

I reached in and grabbed the pills and water, finishing both within seconds.

I hesitated before asking for more water, to which he answered, "Later," and walked away without saying another word.

He disappeared down the hallway, and I said aloud more to myself, "What the hell is going on?! Where is Ashley?"

I searched all over the room for anything that would help me find a way out, knowing well enough that I wouldn't find anything. I approached the glass wall and looked up and down the hallway.

In the direction that Alex disappeared was a flight of stairs leading up, but the staircase turned, obstructing the view of where it led. On the opposite end was a heavy steel door with a small, square, frosted window at the top. There were also four more identical rooms surrounding my room and the one across from mine.

As far as I could tell, they were all empty, but I hoped for a split second that Ashley was in one of them.

"Ashley!" I shouted. "Are you in here?"

"I didn't see anyone else being carried in with you." I heard the soft voice of a man coming from one of the other rooms, but I couldn't tell which one.

"Hello?" I said. "Who was that? Where are you?"

A slender Indian man with scraggly dark hair and a similarly colored wild beard stepped up to the glass in the room closest to the staircase, diagonally across from me. He was wearing wide, black rimmed glasses, which sat upon a nose too big for his thin face.

He looked tired and tepid. If I was right, I knew exactly who this was, but I hoped that I was wrong.

Taking a shot in the dark, I asked, "Amari?"

"Yeah," he said without enthusiasm. "I guess the others know I am missing by now then?"

"Yes."

He mumbled to himself, "They were right then. It worked."

"I'm sorry, what worked?"

"As I'm sure you know, several of us have... well, they're gone..." Amari trailed off.

"Yes?" I offered, encouraging him to continue.

"Peter and Joanna's deaths weren't planned, but Esther and Thomas..." He paused again but continued. "We needed a way to make sure the others knew something was wrong, and they, you know…" He looked at the ground despairingly.

I was speechless and waited for him to continue talking, which took a several minutes.

When he was ready, he explained, "Peter and Joanna were both here about a month before he got me, then a few months later, Peter died after a procedure went wrong. A week after that, Joanna tried to escape when they were bringing her to the back, and they killed her. I was alone after that for a while before he captured Thomas and then Esther."

He took a deep breath and looked at me again before finishing, "We knew that everyone had the visions of Peter and Joanna, and that they would see Thomas and Esther's visions as well. It was Esther's idea. She hoped it would alert the others, causing them to do some searching and trace it back to Alex."

I saw a tear glistening in the corner of his eye at the memory of watching his friends die in front of him.

"Why…" I started to ask but stopped, not sure if it was an appropriate question.

Amari offered an answer anyway, the same question obviously bothering him. "I was younger than them—much younger—and they were willing to sacrifice themselves in the hopes that I would have a chance to live. Esther was sure that help would come once they knew something was wrong."

He added angrily after a moment, nodding his head down the hallway toward the staircase that Alex disappeared onto earlier, "I have my doubts though because no one knows about *him*. However, you're here, and you knew who I was," he said with anticipation.

"I hate to tell you this, but I'm not here on purpose," I admitted. "I honestly wasn't even sure if I believed that we were all in real danger being that I'm new to all of this."

"Great," he said. "Then how did Alex get you in here?"

"He's dating my best friend—has been dating her for months now," I replied. "We were all having drinks and next thing I know, I'm waking up here."

"How did you know who I was then?"

"I met Ben a few months ago, and last time we spoke, he told me Odin couldn't find you. I knew something was off about Alex the last night we were together. Then I pieced it together after waking up down here and seeing you."

"Oh," he answered. "Where are the others?"

"I think all of them are in Logan by now." I looked down and said somberly, "I would've been on my way there now."

We didn't speak for several minutes, though I had many questions. I wasn't sure where to start either. I glanced over at him. His head hung low and pushed up against the glass.

"Amari, don't give up," I said quietly, causing him to look my way. "The others *do* know that something is going on, and soon they'll figure out that I'm missing, too. I'm supposed to check in daily, and Ben knows that I was at Alex's house in Houston. I came here to decide whether I was going to meet up with the others in Logan or stay in New York. Even though he only thinks Alex is my friend's boyfriend, I trust that they'll figure it out."

When he didn't say anything, I wondered how long it would take Ben to realize that I was missing, or if it was possible to escape on our own.

Either way, I decided that I wasn't going to let my story end here in this place. I added determinedly, "We *will* get out of here."

He smiled weakly under the wild beard, and I tried to picture the Amari who wasn't disheveled and hopeless, but rather the sweet, kindhearted guy that Ben described.

"What does Alex want with us anyway? How did you end up here? How does he even know about us?"

"I'm not really sure." I couldn't tell if he was answering all three questions or only one of them, then he added, "We are taken into the lab once a week to have blood drawn and occasionally other tests. No one talks to us or answers any of our questions. At first, Alex would come down to question where the others were—says he will reward us with a week off of tests if we tell him."

My eyes widened and he quickly reassured me by saying that no one had ever given anyone up to Alex. "He also stopped doing that a while back."

"What's your ability?" I asked.

"I can understand and speak any language without studying it."

"That's cool! And useful," I said.

"It's definitely one of the better abilities." He laughed a little to himself. I realized that I still hadn't learned what the rest of the abilities were. "You said you were new... Which one are you?"

"Riley," I answered. "I can hear people's thoughts."

"You're new-new. Peter was a great person," he said. "How did Alex find you so quickly?"

"I have no idea. Like I said before, he's been dating my best friend Ashley since February." It occurred to me that he may have been using Ashley to get to me, or even worse, she was in on it. I brushed the latter thought aside, knowing it was highly unlikely. In addition to being my closest friend, I could hear her thoughts, therefore I would've known if she was assisting Alex.

"He invited us to come stay in Houston for the weekend, and now here I am. I'd literally only met him once before, but Ashley spent so much time with him that I had no reason not to trust her judgement."

A second, awful thought crossed my mind that if he was using her to get to me, maybe he had gotten rid of her after getting what he was really after. Sadly, all I could do right now was hope she was all right.

"Yes, well," Amari said, "he's an excellent liar."

"You never told me how you got trapped in here."

"Oh, right," he stood up straight. "It was sometime last year. I was translating for some businessmen from India at a conference in Atlanta. I met Alex during one of the meetings, and he asked me out for a drink to talk business.

"He seemed like a nice guy and was well admired by all the other businessmen at the conference, so I agreed. While there, he told me how impressed he was with my multilingual skillset, and he wanted to offer me a job which paid double what I was making at the time."

Amari took a deep breath, no doubt feeling foolish for falling for his tricks. He continued anyway. "I was thrilled because someone as successful as him wanted me on their team, but I told him that I needed to think about it. I'd never left India so for me, it was a big decision. For months he took me out to elegant dinners with CEOs, brought me to ball games in box suites, you name it, all to convince me to accept his offer—or so I thought."

"Let me guess, you woke up down here one day..." I suggested.

"Basically." He shrugged his bony shoulders. "We were having drinks one night, and I was getting ready to tell him that I had decided to accept his offer when I blacked out."

"Did you ever tell him about what you were?"

"I've never said a word to anyone, especially him," he said assuredly. "However, he obviously knows what we are. It can't just be a coincidence that he's tracking down and capturing people like us. I just don't know how he knows."

After a moment, he added, "The best I've come up with is that he found out about us and is trying to take our abilities for himself, or he's trying to figure out how to keep himself from aging—maybe both? Seems impossible though, right?"

Twenty-Six

We didn't speak for several minutes while I considered the likelihood that Alex had found a way to steal our abilities or use us to keep himself from aging. I looked over and saw Amari staring blankly at the floor. Before I had the chance to say anything else, Norma stepped out of the doorway at the end of the hall wearing a white lab coat, with Taylor following close behind her, also wearing a similar lab coat.

They both stopped in front of my room, making me take a step backwards.

I glanced at Amari while Norma fumbled with the key in the lock, and he said reassuringly, "It'll be okay. Just don't fight them. It only makes it worse."

My hands were trembling, and my heart was beating fast in my chest. I heeded Amari's advice though and followed them obediently down the hallway and through the door into a lab.

Just like the rooms we were kept in, everything in here was white except for some medical equipment placed neatly in the corner of the room. In the center of the room was a procedure chair, like the ones I remembered seeing at the dentist, except this one had straps on the arm and leg panels.

It'd been a while since I'd been to the dentist, but I didn't remember there ever being straps on the chairs.

"Sit," Norma said curtly.

I looked apprehensively from her to the chair with straps and back again. Norma had a stony look on her face.

As long as you cooperate, we won't need to use those.

I sat down reluctantly, knowing that if there was any chance of Amari and me escaping, fighting against Norma and Taylor wouldn't help.

Norma started with a series of basic tests, taking my temperature, checking blood pressure, evaluating my eyes, ears, nose, and mouth, et cetera. When she was done, Taylor performed vision and hearing tests as she took notes. They both worked silently and methodically, neither in a rush to get me out of there. Once they were both done, Taylor disappeared through a door on the back wall and returned carrying a large needle in one hand and a blood collection bag in the other.

I didn't think he'd care to hear that I didn't like needles, so I squeezed my eyes shut, turned my head away, and took a deep breath as he poked abruptly through the skin on my forearm.

The only question running through my mind the entire time was why Alex would want our blood.

Knowing that I could hear their thoughts, Taylor and Norma remained quiet around me, not wanting to be the ones to reveal his motives. It made me wonder if they worked for Alex out of fear or loyalty.

I felt faint as he removed the needle several minutes later and didn't open my eyes until after he finished wrapping my arm with a bandage.

Norma handed me a granola bar and a glass of water before walking me back to my room.

Once she was gone, Amari asked, "Are you alright?"

"They do that every week?" I asked, ignoring his question and feeling myself becoming exceedingly more outraged at my situation.

"Unfortunately, yes."

Anger spread through me like wildfire. "And you have no idea why?!" The words came out louder than I intended, but I didn't care. Amari knew I wasn't angry with him.

"No." Amari sighed and bowed his head.

***

The following week before my next procedure was like a nightmare that wouldn't end. Time didn't exist down here as there were no windows or clocks. The only concept of time was the lights turning on and off roughly every twelve hours. This I only assumed because shortly after the lights turned on in the morning, Taylor or Norma would bring us breakfast, followed by lunch several hours later, and then dinner. We had a short span of time after dinner before the lights went off again, whether we were ready to go to sleep or not.

Several times I asked if we could each have a book, just to give us something else to do to pass the time, only to be ignored each time.

The worst part by far was not the sheer boredom of being imprisoned down here, but instead it was the suffocating feeling of darkness when the lights shut off at night. There wasn't a single glimmer of light once they were gone to help our eyes adjust. I learned the hard way on the first night to make sure I was in bed before it happened.

We were never taken out of our rooms except for the weekly procedures, so the idea that we could escape on our own faded away with each passing day. I knew Amari had long lost hope of being rescued, but I wasn't giving up that easily.

We talked the most during those few hours of darkness between the lights turning off and one of us falling asleep. I learned a lot about Amari during this time—he seemed happiest when talking about his hometown, family, and the others like us—so I kept him talking in the hopes of boosting his spirits.

He was born in a small coastal town in Odisha, India, in 1926. After his mother died giving birth to him, he was raised by his aunt and uncle. He never knew who his father was until years later, but the man had already passed away by the time he found him.

His aunt and uncle didn't have much money, so they weren't able to provide him with a decent education other than what the local schools offered. After finishing what little school he could, he went on to work on his uncle's farm, saving every bit of money he earned.

"They were kind and loving people," he reminisced. "They always encouraged me to read whatever books I could get my hands on and prayed daily for me that I would make it out of there one day."

He didn't know it at the time, but he received his ability when he turned thirty-one.

"Odin didn't find me for another three years, and since I never ventured out of our region, I never knew that I could understand and speak other languages all of a sudden," he said. "After he explained everything to me, I left my town, my aunt and uncle—everything that I knew—and used my ability to gain better jobs."

After several years of working his way up at a major steel factory in Delhi, he was able to help the company establish themselves in other countries due to his language skills. He became a highly sought after person from then on by other organizations and would move from company to company every ten years or so to avoid questions regarding his unusual youthfulness.

"I never saw my aunt or uncle again after I left them the first time," he said regretfully. "But I always sent money back to them. It was easier that way. After they passed away, I started giving all the money I earned to others or charity. I never needed much. All I wanted was to make a difference and use my ability to help others."

***

When it was time for me to go to the lab again, Taylor and Norma both came to get me from my room and repeated the same tests they did last week, including another blood draw. This second go-round was no better than the first time.

Once we were done, she handed me a granola bar and glass of water, but instead of bringing me back to my room, she said, "Mr. Matthews would like to speak with you."

She and Taylor left through the back door, leaving me alone in the room.

I took this small opportunity to look around the lab in the hopes of finding something that could help us get out of here but found nothing.

I glanced at the medical equipment in the corner of the room. One machine looked like an ultrasound machine and the other was possibly an EKG machine. I got up to look through the drawers of a small cabinet. All I found were neat piles of syringes, needles, towels, specimen cups, cotton swabs, and tongue depressors.

Just as I was closing the top drawer, I heard the knob on the door turn behind me, and I hurried back to the chair in the middle of the room.

Alex entered and rolled a stool next to the procedure chair, his face void of emotion and his dark eyes fixed on mine. The familiar wave of emotions rushed over me, and I felt consumed with lust for him. My body twitched, urging me to be closer to him, the image of our skin touching stuck in my mind.

I tried to fight it, not knowing exactly what it was that I was fighting but knowing that it wasn't real. Then a wave of uncontrollable rage surged through me, making my fists clench into a tight ball.

I realized then that I was not in control of my emotions, but rather he was, though I didn't know how.

Closing my eyes, I yelled as loudly as I could, "Stop!"

When I opened them, he was still watching me but had a manic grin on his face.

"Where is Ashley?" I demanded, feeling as if I was in control of my emotions again.

"Ashley is fine," he said after a moment. "She's back in New York after enjoying the nice, long vacation that you so graciously convinced her to extend."

"Were you just using her to get to me?"

"That was the plan, but I've grown quite fond of her over the last few months. She's... lively." He crossed his legs and placed both hands over one knee. "I may keep her around a little while longer."

"You better not hurt her!" I threatened him, even though we both knew I couldn't do anything if he did hurt Ashley.

He laughed aloud and said, "I never planned on it, but we will see how well you behave yourself."

"Does she know about this?" I asked, gesturing around the room.

"No."

I waited for him to say more and when he didn't, I asked, "What do you want from me? Amari told me that you never talk to us."

"I don't," he stated. "But I have a task for you."

"A task?" I asked dumbfounded.

"Unfortunately, you're so new that you still have ties with too many people and soon, those people are going to start wondering where you are," he said casually. "So, it's simple. All you need to do is tie up a few loose ends, and I'll continue treating your friend like the princess she thinks she is. No one cared that the others went missing. Plus, they were always so troublesome, but then again I never had anything I could use as leverage against them."

My heart sank into my stomach as I processed what he was telling me. He wanted me to make myself disappear so that no one would come looking for me or else he would hurt Ashley. Surely, I thought, he must be bluffing. He wouldn't hurt Ashley, the person he'd been spending so much time with, even if he did just admit that he'd used her to get to me. She was innocent in all of this.

Alex knew what I was thinking because the next thing he said confirmed my thoughts. "I like Ashley, and I don't want to have to hurt her, but I have no problem doing so if you don't cooperate."

After a moment's hesitation I said, "What do you want me to do?"

Alex gave me one day to figure out who I needed to contact and what I would say to each one to make sure they didn't come looking for me. It was the first time that I cried since waking up in this prison one week ago.

The following day, Alex brought me upstairs, to the room that I'd stayed in when Ashley and I first arrived. While I was grateful to see the sun shining outside, everything seemed different now.

The phone was still there, but now there was also a computer sitting on a desk next to the bed that hadn't been here before. He sat down next to me with the intention of monitoring my communications.

"Remember, no tricks, or else Ashley will find herself up against a violent robber on her way home from work," he said without the least bit of sympathy.

The first and easiest was an email to my boss saying that I was quitting my job. I sent a second email to Mark, stating that I decided to move back home and that it would be best if we ended our relationship. I hated myself for breaking up with him over email but I knew that I wouldn't have been able to do so otherwise if I had heard his voice.

Alex sat beside me quietly as I called my mom to tell her that I was fine and that I'd been busy with work. I told her I had a big project that I was working on but that I would call her soon, without any indication of when I would call her again. I almost cried again when I told her that I loved her before hanging up.

My last call was to Ashley at our apartment. I wanted to leave a short message on the machine, because like Mark, I wouldn't be able to lie to her if I heard her voice, and I knew she would find an email from me suspicious. Luckily, she wasn't home, and all I said was that I'd made it to my parents' house and decided to stay a little longer. I didn't make any promises to call her back either.

After I hung up, I looked at Alex, feeling hollow inside. I said, "Happy?"

"Don't be smart," he answered, then added, "Aren't you forgetting one more person?"

My face flushed bright red, but I remained silent.

"Yes, I know all about your little friends in Logan," he said. "Go ahead."

I dialed the familiar phone number and felt my heart pounding in my ears as it rang. A man picked up, but thankfully it wasn't Ben.

"Hi, is Ben there?"

"No, may I ask who's calling?"

"Can you please tell him that Riley called, and that I decided not to come, but I'm okay." I hung up the phone before the man could say anything else.

Alex looked at me for a long time before smiling and saying, "You're different."

How was I different? We were all different if you asked me. Regular people didn't have unnatural abilities like reading minds, superhuman strength, understanding languages you'd never heard and so on.

"How so?" I asked pragmatically.

"You remind me of someone from a long time ago," he responded.

I thought back to Amari's theory that Alex was trying to steal our abilities or keep himself from aging and now I had the feeling that we were way off.

"How long ago?" I asked curiously.

"You're clever too." He looked mildly impressed. "You know, we could make a great team. I could make you more powerful than you can imagine."

I was becoming annoyed with his games and angry that he thought I'd ever consider teaming up with him to do whatever it was he was doing.

"Is that what this is about? Power?"

He paused for a second, considering his next statement. "It's about taking back what is rightfully mine."

"Rightfully yours? How does anything about us have to do with you? And how *do* you know about us?"

"Let me tell you a story," he began. "A long time ago, there were four very powerful brothers and sisters who each ruled one of the four major empires during their time. No one knew where they came from, but people treated them like gods because of their power and immortality. At one point in time, three of the four siblings decided to betray one of the brothers, ultimately causing all four of them to perish. After they were gone, their powers spread evenly amongst their eleven children."

I remained calm as I listened, not believing what he was telling me.

He became indignant as he continued. "No one came before me with my power. I received mine along with my ten cousins after my father was murdered by those foolish people. I know about all of you because I am one of you. An original, if you will. I was the only one clever enough to survive this long, and my father's powers *will* be mine."

EPILOGUE

Ashley let out a deep breath as she stepped into her and Riley's apartment. Her week in Houston with Alex had been perfect. He'd taken her to several amazing restaurants, they toured the Museum of Fine Arts, and she even convinced him to go skinny dipping yesterday after hanging out by his pool all day.

It was nice having someone who treated her like a queen, and she considered herself the luckiest girl in the world. He made her laugh, he was kind and gentle, and he made her feel secure, unlike Nate who only called when he wanted sex. Ashley had told him she loved him one night as they laid in his four-poster king-sized bed, and instead of saying it back, he took her in his arms and made love to her for a second time that night.

She blushed at the memory and felt that she missed him already, but he assured her he'd be back in New York in a couple of days.

The apartment was quieter than usual, and Ashley found herself missing Riley even more. She wondered when she would see her friend again.

She spent most of the day last Sunday being upset with her for leaving without saying goodbye. Alex told Ashley about crossing paths with Riley early that morning where she mentioned she wanted an early start on the road. He explained that Riley said to tell her bye, and she would call soon.

It still didn't make her feel any better, especially since they both passed out early on Saturday night and because she hadn't called yet.

Maybe Riley never made it, she thought.

Ashley looked at the answering machine and saw the light flashing on top, indicating that there was a message.

"See," she said aloud to herself, "that's probably her."

She put her bag on the couch and hit the play button. The first message was from Tuesday morning.

"Hey Riley, it's Ben. I'm just checking in since I haven't heard from you for a couple of days now. I guess you decided to go back to New York, which is fine. Please just give me a call when you can. Thanks."

"That's strange," Ashley said.

Ashley thought that maybe she went home first.

Before she could consider other options, the machine began reading off a second message from yesterday morning.

"Hey, it's me again. It's been a week now since we last spoke. I'm beginning to worry that something happened to you. Please call me. Or if Riley's roommate is hearing this message, call me at..."

Ashley frantically replayed the message to write the number down and dialed it, her hands shaking a little.

"This is Staci," said a woman in a peppy tone.

"Hi, Staci, is Ben available?" Ashley asked, then added, "My name is Ashley."

"One second," Staci set the phone down to where Ashley could still hear voices in the background, including Staci shouting for Ben to pick up the phone.

What seemed like several minutes later, a man with a deep voice picked up the phone and said urgently, "Riley?!"

"No, it's her roommate, Ashley," Ashley answered. "I just got back home and heard your messages... Riley isn't there with you?"

"No, she's not," Ben replied, disappointed. "Did she say she was coming here?"

"Well... yes. She left me in Houston seven days ago to come and see you."

Ben's silence was unnerving, but Ashley waited, trying not to think the worst had happened.

"How much do you know?" he asked calmly.

Ashley hesitated but answered truthfully, "Pretty much everything. How there are others, that none of you age, the dreams, how there is potentially someone out to get all of you."

Ashley could hear him let out his breath, but she couldn't tell if he was angry or relieved that she had a sense of why he was worried.

"She didn't want to tell me, and actually didn't tell me for a long time," Ashley added hastily. "But after the last dream-vision thing she had and you telling her to go to Logan, she didn't know what to do."

"It's okay," Ben said softly. "I'm not mad. I just didn't know how much you knew of the situation."

"Maybe she went home to see her family first..." Ashley offered but was not completely convinced herself.

"Did she say that she may do that?"

"Well, no, but I know it's on her way to Oklahoma, so she possibly made up her mind mid-drive," she said. "I can try to call them if you'd like?"

"No, that's okay," Ben replied. "I don't want to worry them."

"Should I be worried?" Ashley asked after a moment.

"No, we will find her," Ben said confidently. "Thank you for calling, Ashley. I'm sure she's fine—"

Ashley assumed his confidence meant that there had not been any dreams about her.

"—If you hear from her though, please let me know."

"Of course I will!" Ashley said. "And you'll let me know if you find her?"

"Yes, I will."

The call ended, and Ashley sat there, playing last weekend over again in her head, as she was second guessing if Riley had mentioned going home first or not now. No, she thought, Riley specifically said she was going to Logan to be with the others.

She was worried for her friend despite Ben's optimism that they would find her. Although, she found his concern for her well-being comforting.

Still, the only question on her mind was, where was Riley?

Acknowledgements

Thank you to all my family and friends for standing by my side during this long and grueling process, especially my wonderful husband.

Thank you to my editor, who I am so lucky to have partnered with. You took my book to the next level.

Thank you to all the sources on YouTube and Google for providing so much information on self-publishing dos and don'ts.

Thank you to all the coffee shops for the endless supply of caffeine and for being a place I could get away to when I desperately needed to write.

Thank you to the people who pushed me to keep writing, and for all those who are reading this now.

Your love and support means the world to me.

About the Author

Gena Gendusa LaSalle is a coffee enthusiast, avid reader, keeper of many animals, and an aspiring, green-thumbed gardener. She's a native to South Louisiana where she works alongside her brother and sister at their family-owned insurance agency. She loves spending her spare time with her husband and daughter on their small homestead in the country.

If she's not reading a book, she's working on writing one. Gena has previously published a short children's Christmas book and is currently working on books two and three of the *Black Horse* series.

Gena's love for books goes back to reading *Junie B. Jones* in elementary school and spending way too much piggy-bank money at the book fair. The idea of writing her own book came much later in life after coming up with the idea on a road trip.